DOCTOR WHO

REMEMBRANCE OF THE DALEKS

The Doctor Who *50th Anniversary Collection*

Ten Little Aliens
Stephen Cole

Dreams of Empire
Justin Richards

Remembrance of the Daleks
Ben Aaronovitch

EarthWorld
Jacqueline Rayner

Only Human
Gareth Roberts

Beautiful Chaos
Gary Russell

The Silent Stars Go By
Dan Abnett

BBC

DOCTOR WHO

REMEMBRANCE OF THE DALEKS

BEN AARONOVITCH

BBC
BOOKS

3 5 7 9 10 8 6 4

First published in 1990 by WH Allen & Co plc.
This edition published in 2013 by BBC Books, an imprint of Ebury Publishing.
A Random House Group Company

Doctor Who is a BBC Wales production for BBC One.
Executive producers: Steven Moffat and Caroline Skinner

The Random House Group Limited Reg. No. 954009
Addresses for companies within the Random House Group can be found at
www.randomhouse.co.uk

A CIP catalogue record for this book is available from the British Library.

ISBN 978 1 849 90598 5

Editorial director: Albert DePetrillo
Editorial manager: Nicholas Payne
Series consultant: Justin Richards
Project editor: Steve Tribe
Cover design: Two Associates © Woodlands Books Ltd, 2012
Production: Alex Goddard

Printed and bound in Great Britain by Clays Ltd, St Ives plc

To buy books by your favourite authors and register for offers,
visit www.randomhouse.co.uk

INTRODUCTION

When *Doctor Who* script editor Andrew Cartmel told me that publisher WH Allen would, perforce, offer me first refusal on the novelisation of *Remembrance of the Daleks*, I was filled with enthusiasm. Hurrah, I thought, not only did I luck into writing the Daleks on my first ever TV gig but I also get paid to learn how to write prose. It never occurred to me that turning my script into 40,000+ words, roughly twenty times the maximum length of any other of my prose outings, would prove difficult. I charged in with all the empty-headed mad enthusiasm of youth. Like many a first work, my novelisation can be seen as an amalgam of diverse influences, most of them from science fiction. Consequently, there are the portentous quotes from imaginary books, à la Frank Herbert, the supercharged cyberpunk imagery of the Dalek-on-Dalek battles, cf. William Gibson, and the flash memories by characters in extremis which I'm fairly certain I lifted from somewhere, even if I can't remember exactly where.

Producer John Nathan Turner, catching wind of my reckless charge into the literary breach, asked me to at least try and make sure it matched the TV episodes as they were broadcast. There was a plaintive note in his voice – I think he had been burnt before.

One thing was certain, it wasn't simply going to be the script with 'he said' or 'she said' added at the end of each line of dialogue. My characters were going to have an interior life and my fictional worlds would have some depth. Well, perhaps not depth exactly, but definitely not suitable for unaccompanied children under five.

It never occurred to me to do it any other way.

Fortunately there were precedents, and indeed precedents that I was familiar with from my childhood, in the form of the novelisations by Malcolm Hulke. I was given a copy of *Doctor Who and the Doomsday Weapon* (adapted by Hulke from his own screenplay *Colony in Space*) by my mum. She approved of Hulke because she knew him through the Party (that's the Communist Party of Great Britain, by the way), which outweighed the fact that the book was science fiction – a genre she despised.

Hulke, too, had imbued his characters with backstory (particularly the evil commander) and beefed up the special effects while retaining both the form and spirit of his story. With his example in mind, I plunged into my first serious venture into prose. In the process I learnt two important lessons. One was that 40,000 is really a large number of words while, weirdly, not really being enough. The other was that the biggest difference between prose and scripts is the way you handle transitions from scene to scene. In TV you can rely on the visual cues to tell the audience who's in a particular scene, but in prose you've got to find ways to remind the reader who is in the scene and, more importantly, who exactly the scene is focused on, dramatically speaking, and why the reader should care about them.

I haven't read *Remembrance of the Daleks* since it came out in the early 1990s. I find it hard to read my own work, and in any case I'm never objective about its quality. I thought the book was good stuff when I wrote it, and it was well received and people seem to enjoy it. Which is all you can ask for in a piece of work.

And it did teach me to write prose – or at least point me in the right direction.

So, if you plan to read the rest of this book, I hope you will be gentle in your judgement of it. It was my first time, and if it seems a bit rushed, a bit earnest — and occasionally up itself unto its third knuckle – then there's a simple reason for that.

If you can't be all those things when you're young – what's the point?

Ben Aaronovitch
August 2012

I, that am curtail'd of this fair proportion,
Cheated of feature by dissembling nature,
Deform'd, unfinish'd, sent before my time
Into this breathing world, scarce half made up,
And that so lamely and unfashionable
That dogs bark at me, as I halt by them;
Why, I, in this weak piping time of peace,
Have no delight to pass away the time.

Richard III, I.i

PROLOGUE

The old man had a shock of white hair pulled back from a broad forehead; startling eyes glittered in a severe high-cheekboned face. Although he was stooped when he walked, his slim body hinted at hidden strengths. Light from the streetlamps, blurred by the gathering mist, glinted in the facets of the blue gem set in the ring on his finger.

He paused for bearings by a pair of gates on which the words:

I M FOREMAN
Scrap Merchant

were barely visible in the night, before carefully picking his way through the junkyard towards the police box at its centre.

A common enough sight in the England of the early 1960s, the dark blue police box was strangely out of place in the junkyard, and even more oddly, this one was humming. The old man stopped by its doors and reached into a pocket for the key.

'There you are, grandfather,' said a girl's voice from inside.

His sharp hearing picked up a woman's whispered

response from behind him. 'It's Susan,' said the woman.

The old man's face creased with irritation as he sensed that he was about to be delayed for a long time. But then time was relative, especially to someone such as himself.

1

One, two, three, four,
Who's that knocking at the door?
Five, six, seven, eight,
It's the Doctor at the gate.

Children's skipping chant

'What's she staring at?' demanded Ace, balefully staring at one of the many girls that clustered around the entrance to Coal Hill School.

'Your clothing is little anachronistic for this period,' said the Doctor, 'and that doesn't help.'

Ace defensively hefted the big black Ono-Sendai tape deck to a more nonchalant position on her shoulder and continued to stare at the girl. Nobody outstares me, she thought, especially some twelve-year-old sprat in school uniform. The girl turned away.

'Hah,' exclaimed Ace with satisfaction, and turned her attention to the Doctor. 'Is it my fault that this decade's got no street cred?' Ace waited for a reaction from the Doctor, but she got nothing. He seemed to be gazing intently at a squat ugly van parked opposite the school.

'Strange,' murmured the Doctor.

'Oi, Professor. Can we get something to eat now?'

The Doctor, however, was oblivious to Ace's question. 'Very odd.'

'Professor?

The Doctor finally shifted his attention to Ace. His eyes travelled suspiciously to her rucksack. 'You haven't got any explosives in there have you?'

'No.' Ace braced herself for the 'gaze'. The Doctor's strange intense eyes swept over her and then away. Ace slowly let out her breath – the 'gaze' had passed on.

'What do you make of that van?'

Ace dutifully considered the van. It was a Bedford, painted black, with sliding doors and a complicated aerial sprouting from the roof.

'Dunno,' she shrugged. 'TV detector van? Professor, I'm starving to death.'

The Doctor was unmoved by Ace's plea for ~nance. He shook his head. 'Wrong type of aerial for t. No, for this time period that's a very sophisticated piece of equipment.'

In this decade, thought Ace, a crystal set is a sophisticated piece of equipment. 'What's so sophisticated about that? I've seen CBs with better rigs. I'm hungry.'

'You shouldn't have disabled the food synthesizer then,' retorted the Doctor.

'I thought it was a microwave.'

'Why would you put plutonium in a microwave?'

'I didn't know it was plutonium, you shouldn't leave that stuff lying around.'

'What did you think it was then?'

'Soup.'

'Soup?'

'Soup. I'm still hungry – lack of food makes me hungry you know.'

'Lack of food makes you obstreperous.' The Doctor applied his much vaunted mind to the problem. 'Why don't you go and buy some consumables? There's a cafe down there.' He gestured down the alley where they had landed the TARDIS. 'Meanwhile I will go and undertake a detailed and scientific examination of that van which has so singularly failed to grab your attention.'

'Right,' Ace turned and walked away, feeling the 'gaze' on her back. The Doctor called after her and she turned sharply.

'What?'

'Money,' said the Doctor holding out a drawstring purse.

Just what did I think they were going to take, thought Ace as she took the purse, Iceworld saving coupons? 'Thanks.'

The Doctor smiled.

From the gateway of the school the sandy haired girl that had earlier stared at Ace watched as she turned and walked away.

Ace followed the alley until it came out onto Shoreditch High Road. Across the road and facing her was the cafe. A sign above the window proclaimed it as Harry's Cafe.

Food at last, thought Ace.

Sergeant Mike Smith pushed his plate to one side,

leaned back in his chair and turned to the sports page of the *Daily Mirror*. The jukebox whirred a record into place, the tea urn steamed, and the music started.

Mike luxuriated in the cold weather, his memories of the wet, green heat of Malaya fading among the cracked lino and fried food smell of Harry's Cafe. He was content to let them go, and allow the East End to bring him home from the heat and boredom of those eighteen months abroad.

The cafe door banged open and a girl walked in. Mike glanced up at a flash of black silk – the girl was wearing a black silk jacket with improbable badges pinned or stitched to the arms. She shrugged a rucksack off her shoulders revealing the word 'Ace' stitched into the back. Something that surely could not be a transistor radio was dumped casually on a nearby table.

The girl approached the counter.

Mike watched as she leaned over the counter and looked around. She didn't move like any girl he knew, and certainly she didn't dress like anybody he had ever seen.

She banged her knuckles on the worn Formica counter.

'Hallo,' she called. Her accent was pure London.

The Doctor frowned at the aerial. It represented an intrusion into his plans and the implications of that worried him. He noticed a ladder giving access to the roof of the van and within moments he stood there, balanced perfectly by the aerial. One part of his mind solved a series of equations dealing with angles, displacement, and the optimum wavelength, while another part of his mind began re-examining important aspects of the plan.

The first answer came swiftly; the second cried out for more data. The Doctor sighed: sometimes intuition, even his, had limitations. Quickly sighting down the length of the aerial, he looked up... to find himself staring at the menacing Victorian bulk of Coal Hill School.

Ace banged the counter again. 'Hallo,' she yelled, louder than intended. 'Service? Anybody home?' There was no response.

'Not like that,' said a man's voice.

Ace twisted round sharply to find a young man standing close to her – far too close. Ace backed off a little, gaining some space. 'Like what, then?'

The man grinned, showing good teeth. His eyes were blue and calculating. 'Like this,' he said and turning to look over the counter bellowed parade-ground style: 'Harry, customer!' He turned back to Ace who cautiously removed her hands from her ears. 'Like that.'

A voice answered from the back of the cafe.

'See,' said the man, leaning in again, 'easy when you know how.'

A short squat man with the face of a boxer emerged from the depths of the cafe. Presumably this was Harry. 'Give it a rest, Mike,' he said to the younger man, who laughed and went back to his table. 'I had enough of that in the war.'

Harry turned to Ace. 'Can I help you miss?'

Ace considered the state of her stomach. 'Four bacon sandwiches and a cup of coffee, please.'

The Doctor stepped carefully through the gate, dodging children who were eager to be rid of their school. Drained of its inmates Coal Hill School loomed dour as a prison over the deserted playground.

Movement caught the Doctor's eye. The girl who had been watching Ace was there, chanting as she skipped from one chalked box to another. Around her, black circles were etched into the concrete. The four of them were in a square pattern like the pips on a die. With a quick sideways lunge the Doctor stepped close to the marks and stooped, running a finger along one of them. The finger came up black, sooty with carbonized concrete.

He looked up at the girl and for a moment their eyes met; then she whirled and was gone.

Rachel was lost in the mechanics of detection. The interior of the van was cramped with equipment, casting bulky shadows in the glow from the cathode ray tube. For a second she lost the signal in the clutter caused by the surrounding buildings, but with deft movements she refocused. There, got it, she thought. Behind her the back doors opened and the van rocked as someone climbed in. She knew it would be Sergeant Smith.

Rachel kept her eyes on the screen. 'You took your time. Get on the radio and tell the group captain,' she looked back, 'I think I've located the…'

Intense grey eyes met her own.

'Source of a magnetic fluctuation, perhaps?' the man asked helpfully, his extraordinary eyes darting over the instruments.

She heard herself answering as if from a distance. 'A rhythmical pulsed fluctuation, yes.' She had the sudden bizarre impression that she was superfluous to the conversation and that the man with the odd eyes already knew the answers.

Reaching out he casually adjusted the tuning so that the image on the oscilloscope resolved into steady jagged peaks. 'I rather thought so. No possibility of it being a natural phenomenon?'

'Not likely. It's a repeated sequence,' she said. 'It must be artificial in origin.'

'Yes.'

Reality began to creep in at the edges of Rachel's perception and only then she realized how clouded her mind had become. 'Excuse me?'

The man looked up. 'Yes.'

'Who are you?'

'I'm the Doctor.' He extended his hand and Rachel shook it; his palm was cool.

'I'm Rachel, Professor Rachel Jensen.'

'Pleased to meet you.' There was a flash of recognition. 'You know, I'm sure I've heard of you.'

There were questions Rachel knew she should be asking, but as they faced each other nose to nose, nothing came to mind.

The radio buzzed, breaking the silence. Rachel grabbed her headset desperately. It was Allison, the physicist seconded from Cambridge.

'Red Four receiving.'

Allison's voice came over the headphones, quavering in panic. 'Red Six, we're under attack…'

Walking back through the alley, Mike was trying to explain the intricacies of British currency to Ace.

'Let me get this straight,' said Ace, 'twelve pennies to the shilling, eight shillings to the pound…'

'No,' said Mike, stepping around a police box that half blocked the alley. 'Twenty shillings to the pound.' He was sure that police box hadn't been there before.

'Stupid system,' said Ace.

'Where are you from?'

'Perivale. Why?'

Mike considered her reply – wasn't that up west somewhere, past Shepherd's Bush? 'Just wondered.'

'If it's twenty shillings to the pound, and that means two hundred and forty pence to the pound,' she looked at Mike for confirmation, and he nodded, 'then what's half a crown?'

Before Mike could answer he heard someone calling him. He looked ahead for the van. Professor Jensen was beside it, waving. 'Sergeant,' she called on seeing him, 'we have to get moving.'

Mike started towards her. 'What is it?'

Professor Jensen shouted something about the group captain and something about Matthews. Mike closed the gap between himself and the van.

'The group captain said he's under attack. Matthews is hurt.'

Mike yanked back the sliding door and jumped into

the driver's seat. 'Where are they?' he asked as Rachel got in beside him.

'At the secondary source, Foreman's Yard. It's just off Totters Lane – did you hear that?'

'What?' asked Mike as he turned the ignition key. The engine caught first time.

'I thought I heard the back doors slamming.'

'Hold on,' said Mike and slammed his foot down hard on the accelerator.

In the back of the van, Ace looked at the Doctor. She had learnt that wherever they were, in whatever bizarre circumstances, the Doctor at least was consistent.

She had been walking up the alley with Mike before he had run off, and then the Doctor had appeared between the open back doors of the van and called to her.

Ace had jumped in without hesitating, the Doctor had slammed the doors, and the van had accelerated – Ace figured Mike was in the front. She had lost her grip on her food in the confusion.

'What's going on?' she asked the Doctor.

'Adventure,' said the Doctor, holding up a packet of bacon sandwiches, 'excitement, that sort of thing.'

2
FRIDAY, 16:03

Mike swore as he pressed down on the brake pedal. A long greasy plume of smoke, its base hidden by a wall of civilians, rose above Totters Lane.

'Foreman's Yard,' said Rachel, pointing. 'There, the entrance is behind those people.'

Mike carefully nosed the van through the crowd, flashing his identity card at a policeman, who let them through the gates.

The yard was littered with rusty iron and industrial debris; the smoke was coming from a shabby lean-to at one end.

Mike stopped the van and got out. To his left Group Captain Gilmore draped a blanket over a body. Gilmore looked up as Mike and Rachel approached.

'What's the situation?' said a voice behind them.

Mike turned and saw Ace with a strange little man.

'Who the devil are you?' demanded Gilmore.

'I'm the Doctor,' said the man, nodding at Professor Jensen.

Gilmore rounded on Jensen. 'Is he with you?'

Mike watched while Rachel hesitated for a moment, her eyes locked on the Doctor's.

'Yes,' she answered, 'he's with me.'

Gilmore snorted and caught sight of Ace. 'Sergeant,'

he snapped at Mike. 'Take the girl and set up a position at Red Six.'

Mike quickly saluted and, gesturing to Ace, took off for Red Six, the other detector van. He was grateful that the group captain had been too busy to ask who Ace was and just what she had been doing in the back of the van – questions that Mike would like answered himself.

Was that wise? Rachel asked herself as she knelt by the body with the Doctor and Gilmore. She watched as the Doctor pulled back the blanket. Matthews' dead face stared up at her: his skin was pale and clammy, webbed with broken capillaries. Now what caused that I wonder? thought Rachel.

The Doctor opened the dead man's shirt and carefully pressed down with his hands.

'No visible tissue damage,' he said. Something gave under his hands. 'Ah,' he pressed down in a new pattern, 'massive internal displacement.'

'What?' asked Gilmore.

'His insides were scrambled,' said the Doctor, 'very nasty.'

There's an understatement, thought Rachel. 'Concussion effect?' she asked.

'No, a projected energy weapon.'

A what? Rachel was puzzled.

'A projected what?' demanded Gilmore.

'A death ray?' demanded Rachel.

'Exactly,' said the Doctor. 'I hope you have reinforcements coming.'

'Any minute now. But this is preposterous,' protested

Gilmore. 'A death ray – it's unbelievable.'

Allison Williams stared at Mike. 'Dead? Are you sure?' she asked for the third time.

Mike nodded. He noticed Ace staring back to where the group captain, Professor Jensen and the Doctor were examining the body. He'd liked Matthews, and now Matthews was dead. It had happened like that before in Malaya.

The Doctor crouched behind the remains of a boiler, flakes of red paint rough under his hands. He looked towards the lean-to. 'Whatever fired the weapon is trapped in there. There's no way out.'

Gilmore, his doubts about death rays notwithstanding, kept down and followed the Doctor's gaze. 'How can you be sure?'

'I've been here before.'

Rachel heard the roar of a large engine behind her. Turning she saw the big khaki Bedford draw into the yard.

'Good,' said Gilmore with evident satisfaction, 'we'll have him out in a jiffy.'

Private Abbot snapped out of sleep as he felt a sharp pain in his left shin. Amery, opposite, grinned at him. The truck had stopped. He nudged Bellos, beside him.

'Where are we?' he asked.

The big Yorkshireman shrugged. 'London.'

'Clever.'

Somebody banged hard on the truck's side board. 'All

right boys, let's be having you,' yelled Sergeant Embery from outside.

Grabbing their guns the squad scrambled out of the truck. Abbot heard Bellos swear and the crunch of grit as his feet hit concrete. Out of habit he scanned the area: it was a rectangular yard with rusty scrap for cover. He didn't like cover as it could hide snipers, especially in the buildings that framed two sides of the yard.

Abbot felt an odd tension in his gut as Embery ordered them into parade formation. Special duties, easy posting – this is London ain't it? he thought. Smoke rose from a lean-to in the far corner. That suggested a bomb.

'It's Chunky,' said Bellos as the group captain came forward. On the command, Abbot came to attention with the rest of the squad.

Gilmore ran a practised eye over the squad as he outlined the position. Detailing Sergeant Embery to take two men and clear the onlookers from around the gate, he called Mike over. 'Take two men and get Matthews away from there.'

Mike picked two men and led them away.

'I'm not sure you know what you're dealing with,' said the Doctor.

'I assure you, Doctor,' anger made his voice clipped, 'these are picked men; they can deal with anything.' He looked again at the veil of smoke obscuring the lean-to. 'Providing they can see it.'

The warrior had been dormant for a while. Delicate

sensors passed information through a spun web of crystal and laser light, down into the breathing heart of itself where its intelligence sat. The data resolved itself into a concept, mapped out in three-dimensional space.

Figures moved in and out of perspective, and as activity increased, the manner in which they moved became decisive. Fast motions activated subroutines which awoke dormant systems and made demands on the warrior's central power reserve – demands that were met.

The focus of the warrior's attention sharpened, shooting into the infra-red spectrum. The figures became luminous, shifting patches of red; they carried hard metal objects which in a nanosecond the battle computer identified as weapons.

Tracking systems warmed up and the warrior shifted power to its blaster.

Mike caught the flash of light in the periphery of his vision. His mind still registered it as a muzzle flash even as his eyes showed it moving. One of the soldiers with him was caught as he stooped over Matthews' body, caught and whirled backwards to sprawl brokenly in the dust. The air carried the sharp tang of ozone.

A man was down, provoking Gilmore to shout for covering fire. Around Rachel soldiers scrambled into position while others opened up with their rifles. She had seen it: her eyes had been looking at the lean-to when the bolt of energy had shot out. It was like a bolt of lightning, but…

Ace could hear screams from the crowd at the gate

over the sound of the gunfire. Puffs of dust peppered the walls around the lean-to as the bullets left saucer-shaped depressions in the brick. She saw the Doctor crouched behind an old boiler. She tried to make out his expression; Ace thought she saw self-disgust for a moment before the Doctor's face became grim, his eyes flat.

Group Captain Gilmore, unable to see a target, ordered his men to cease firing. In the sudden quiet he could hear the muted roar of traffic. To the left of Matthews another man lay dead. It looked like MacBrewer: Catholic, married, four children, career soldier, dead in the dust of an east London junkyard. A sudden debilitating rage filled Gilmore and with it foreboding.

'What was it?' Professor Jensen demanded behind him.

A second voice, the Doctor who had arrived with her. 'That was your death ray.'

'I know that, but how?' Jensen's voice was sharp. 'To transmit focused energy at that level, it's incredible, it's...' her voice trailed off.

Gilmore turned to face them. Jensen looked uncertain, as if she were struggling with something unacceptable.

'Yes?' asked the Doctor, his eyes bright.

'It's beyond the realm of current technology.' Jensen had to force the words out.

Enough of this, Gilmore thought angrily. 'We can save the science lecture for a less precipitous moment. Now, Doctor, if you can just tell me what's going on?'

'You must pull your men back,' he said quickly. 'Now.

It's their only chance.'

'Preposterous, we can't disengage now. Whatever is in there, these men can deal with it.' But he was uncertain even as he spoke. Who is this man and what does he know? he asked himself. He heard the Doctor speaking even as he made his decision.

'Nothing you have will be effective against what's in there.'

We'll see about that, thought Gilmore. He summoned Sergeant Embery and told him to fire three rifle grenades on even spread directly into the lean-to. Let's see what this damned sniper makes of that, he thought.

Why does he refer to the sniper as an it? Rachel pondered as she watched the Doctor rally his arguments one more time. Who or what could wield such an energy weapon?

'Group Captain,' pleaded the Doctor, 'you are not dealing with human beings here.'

'What am I dealing with – little green men?'

'No,' answered the Doctor. 'Little green blobs in bonded polycarbide armour.'

Embery reported that the grenades were ready.

'Fire!' ordered Gilmore.

Rachel watched as the Doctor turned away. 'Humans,' he said disgustedly.

Abbot felt the kick as the grenade was knocked forward by the rifle round. He watched with a practised eye the blurred trajectory of the grenade which hit the entrance of the shed dead centre. Fire blossomed a moment later.

Ace watched the explosions rack the shed reducing

it to a ragged, debris-strewn cave. The size of the blast indicated a fairly low-grade explosive core wrapped in a fragmentation shell; she would have to acquire one to make sure.

She rushed over to the Doctor.

'Did you see that, Professor?' she said as she reached him. 'Unsophisticated but impressive,' she added airily. The Doctor, however, ignored her.

Gilmore looked with grim satisfaction at the remains of the lean-to. 'I believe that should do the trick,' he said to the Doctor.

The girl in the strange jacket was staring at the wreckage. The enthusiasm on her face disturbed Gilmore: he was reminded of France in 1944 and the two German soldiers his men had scraped off the interior of a pillbox.

Sergeant Smith was hovering waiting to do something. Gilmore ordered him to call up further reinforcements and an ambulance. The Doctor frowned at this and told him that reinforcements weren't going to make any difference.

'My men have just put three fragmentation grenades into a confined space; nothing even remotely human could have survived that.'

The Doctor's eyes fixed on Gilmore's. 'That's the point, Group Captain,' the Doctor said softly. 'It isn't even remotely human.'

The warrior's sensors were still flaring from the aftermath of the explosions. A blizzard of metal had engulfed it; there was damage, but it was minor – only chips off its armour. It quickly sought to regain its perception of the outside world.

The first data came from modulated signals in the low frequency electromagnetic spectrum. The battle computer identified them as communications: the enemy was seeking to communicate, perhaps with its gestalt, probably ordering up more forces. Target-seeking routines locked on to the source; infra-red detectors once more probed through the wall of smoke.

A primitive vehicle was the source. The warrior could make out the shifting blur of an enemy partly masked by the cold metal. A data search lasting nanoseconds brought priorities: neutralize communications, destroy the force opposing it, crush all resistance, obliterate the enemy for the glory of the race. Fulfilment of its function brought a strange excitement within the warrior's twisted body.

A very real and terrible emotion.

Mike was out of the van and in the air before any details of the attack registered: a bang, glass in the side window shattering, the radio handset slapped out of his hands, the smell of ozone, and the ground slowly rising to meet him as he dived out of the open door. He tucked in his head and felt the world roll over his shoulders; he could smell the dust of the yard. Mike snapped to his feet still holding his submachine-gun.

Private John Lewis Abbot counted himself an old soldier at twenty-six years of age and definitely planned to live long enough to fade away. The rest of the squad shared this ambition. To them hostile fire was hostile fire, whether it was a machine-gun round or a funny looking bolt of lightning, and everyone dived for cover and then blazed away in the direction of the enemy until Gilmore yelled at them to wait for a target. Abbot crouched down, snapped a new clip of ammunition into his rifle and carefully sighted down the barrel, waiting for a target.

Then it came.

It was grey and metallic, a stunted thing that glided with ugly grace out of the smoke. A tube protruding from the smooth top dome swung deliberately from side to side. Energy belched from a gun-stick midway down the thing's body.

It was a target and Abbot fired.

The FN-FAL automatic rifle is a Belgian design which weighs 4.98 kilograms loaded and fires a full-sized cartridge. The 7.62 millimetre bullet leaves the muzzle at 2756 feet per second and has an effective range of 650 metres; at close range the bullet can pass through a concrete wall. In accordance with British military doctrine that an aimed round is worth twenty fired rapidly, the FN-FAL used by the RAF Regiment fires single shots only – one squeeze on the trigger, one carefully aimed round fired.

In the first second of the firefight the target was struck at close range by seventy-three carefully aimed rounds. The bullets bounced off the target's armour to ricochet uselessly into the junkyard.

'Give me some of that nitro-nine you're not carrying,' said the Doctor. Ace unpacked what looked like a grey can of deodorant from her rucksack and passed it over. The Doctor looked anxiously over his shoulder. 'Another,' he demanded.

'It's my last can.'

'I should hope so too. The fuse, how long?'

'Ten seconds.'

'Long enough!'

Rachel ducked as a bolt of energy blew a hole in a bit of nearby machinery and shrapnel whined over her head. Cautiously she looked over the bonnet of the Bedford. It has to be a machine, she reasoned, perhaps a sort of remote-controlled tank. The stalk at the top had to be a camera, but the weapon... a light-maser, but how many megawatts would it take to generate a beam?

The thing fired again, and this time Rachel traced the path of the bolt. I can see it moving, it can't be coherent light. Perhaps it's superheated plasma? She continued to search for an explanation.

Gilmore yelled over the noise at her: 'When I tell you, take the girl and make for the gate.'

A man shrieked somewhere off to the right.

Gilmore frowned as he pushed shells into his revolver, then, bracing his arms on the bonnet, he looked over his shoulder. 'Now, Rachel, go!'

It wasn't until later that Rachel realized that Gilmore had called her by her first name.

Gilmore was about to fire when he saw the Doctor running forward. Ducking round a metal pillar the Doctor whistled at the squat metal machine. 'Oi, Dalek,' he shouted, 'over here. It's me, the Doctor!'

Gilmore watched in horror as the eyestalk swivelled to focus on the Doctor, who seemed to be pulling the tops off a pair of aerosol cans. The machine had paused as if it were uncertain.

'What's the matter with you?' the Doctor shouted irritably. 'Don't you recognize your sworn enemy?'

Ducking, the Doctor placed the cans by a large stack of bricks. As the machine moved towards him, the Doctor crept away towards Gilmore's position.

Three.

A quiver of anticipation ran through the warrior as its battle computer verified the data. Desire ran hot through sluggish veins, its internal life support compensating for the sudden demand on blood sugar. There was a high probability that this was the Doctor, the *Ka Faraq Gatri* – the enemy of the Daleks.

Four.

The Doctor desperately zigzagged as bolts of energy flared around him…

Five

… reproaching himself for being in this ridiculous situation, he decided to blame the human race for it…

Six.

… rather then worry about the homicidal Dalek behind him…

Seven.

… or the vagaries of Ace's chemistry or how many red bricks it takes to crack a Dalek or…

A kilogram of nitro-nine exploded eight metres behind him.

Luckily the ground broke his fall.

He stayed where he was, his eyes focused on the dirt in front of his face: there he noticed two ants fighting for possession of a tiny fragment of leaf.

Ace was shouting somewhere. Feet thundered towards the Doctor, and then hands tugged at his arm. Sighing quietly he rose to his feet. Ace was bounding agitatedly at his elbow. 'You said ten seconds,' he said slowly.

'No one's perfect, Professor.' She moved back as the Doctor violently brushed dust off his coat. 'Are you all right?'

'Of course.' He sounded surprised. 'Can you drive a truck?'

'Why?'

'Good, I thought so. Come on.'

The machine lay cracked open. Something green oozed between shattered metal and bits of brick. Rachel started towards it.

'I want a full emergency team here on the double,' Gilmore was telling Mike behind her. 'And put a guard on this site. I want a weapons team at Coal Hill School and I want them armed with ATRs.'

Mike answered and left.

Rachel carefully removed a chunk of brick from the upper casing; a fetid odour of zinc and vinegar invaded her nose. Allison passed her a metal probe which she used to poke out a sample of tissue.

'It has an organic component.'

'Or an occupant,' said Allison.

'What the devil is it?' asked Gilmore.

'A Dalek,' said the Doctor.

Ace gave the ignition key another savage twist, cursing stone-age technology under her breath.

'Trouble is, it's the wrong Dalek.'

Aced looked over the primitive dashboard, hunting for something to start the van. 'What would the right Dalek be like? Better or worse?'

'Guess.'

The engine turned over and juddered to a stop.

'Choke,' said the Doctor.

'No thanks.'

The Doctor reached over and pulled out a knob on the dashboard. Ace turned the key and the engine revved up. Ace made a stab at the gears and the van lurched forward. The driver's door slammed backwards and Mike angrily stuck in his head.

'Oi!' he shouted over the engine noise. 'What are you doing?'

'Borrowing your van,' the Doctor said cheerily as Ace put her foot down and the van roared away. Ace caught a glimpse of Mike's astonished face as she veered the van out of the junkyard and left into Totters Lane.

'These Dahliks?'

'Daleks,' the Doctor corrected.

'Daleks, whatever. Where are they from?'

'Skaro. Left here.'

'When were they left here?'

'No, no,' cried the Doctor, 'turn left here.'

'Right,' Ace heaved on the steering wheel and sent the van careering down a narrow street. That's funny, thought Ace, I didn't know they had one-way systems in 1963. Oncoming traffic started to behave in a peculiar manner.

'Concentrate on where you're going,' shouted the Doctor.

'I'm doing the best I can,' Ace yelled. A narrow railway bridge loomed in front of them. 'If you don't like it, you drive.'

The van plunged into darkness.

They emerged into the light and the Doctor was driving. Ace stared at his umbrella which she was now holding. The seats, dashboard and steering wheel were all in the right positions – it was just that the Doctor was sitting behind the wheel and Ace was in the passenger seat. I think I'll just decide that never happened, she decided.

'The Daleks,' resumed the Doctor, 'are the mutated remains of a race called the Kaleds.'

The Doctor remembered that time when he stepped out of a petrified forest and saw a city of metal spread out under an alien sky. He thought of Temmosus, the Thal leader, screaming for peace and friendship even as a Dalek gunned him down. Images of people, the last desperate rush to thwart the Dalek's plan to mine the Earth's core. Crawling among the thousands of dormant warriors in the ice caves of Spiridon, and then later, the Time Lords' intervention and Davros.

'The Kaleds were at war with the Thals. They had a dirty nuclear war in which evolution of the resulting mutations was accelerated by the Kaleds' chief scientist Davros. What he created he placed in metal war machines and that is how the Daleks came about.'

His mind again went back to Skaro, a planet wasted

and broken by a centuries-long conflict – all rubble, death and mutations. From the debris rose the stench of corruption: Davros, rotting and grotesque, gloating over the death of his own people. 'The Daleks will be all powerful! They will bring peace throughout the galaxy, they are the superior beings.'

'So that metal thing had a creature inside controlling it?' asked Ace.

'Exactly. Ever since their creation the Daleks have been attempting to conquer and enslave as much of the universe as they could get their grubby little protruberances on.'

'And they want to conquer the Earth?'

'Nothing so mundane. They conquer the Earth in the 22nd century. No, they want the Hand of Omega.'

'The what?'

But the Doctor had said enough for the moment. 'One thing at a time, Ace. First we have to discover what's going on at the school.'

3
FRIDAY, 17:30

UNIT had its roots in the Intrusion Counter Measures Group established in 1961, under the command of Group Captain Ian Gilmore of the newly formed Royal Air Force Regiment. Staffed with Royal Air Force personnel it was charged with the task of protecting the UK from covert actions by hostile powers and mounting intelligence operations against such a threat. In 1963 it was involved in what later came to be known as the Shoreditch Incident, details of which have never emerged, even to this day.

The Zen Military – A History of UNIT
by Kadiatu Lethbridge-Stewart (2006)

Maybury Hall was a sprawling red brick building near the Hendon base. It was usually used for recreation, but Group Captain Gilmore had requisitioned it as his headquarters. Now in the billiard room the portrait of the Queen looked down on teleprinters, radios and field telephones; in the officer's club the lower ranks sat with feet up on oak tables and stubbed out Woodbines in crystal ashtrays.

Gilmore decided that he needed a field base closer to

the area of operations. Sergeant Smith might be able to help on that: Smith had connections in the Shoreditch area, like that man Ratcliffe. Smith had brought him in, a short, broad-shouldered man with the unmistakable bearing of a soldier. Smith said that Ratcliffe ran the Shoreditch Association and that the manpower it could mobilize would be useful to them for ancillary tasks. Gilmore had agreed to notify him if they were needed. Something, however, nagged at Gilmore's memory: Ratcliffe – I've heard that name before. But he had far more important things to occupy him.

George Ratcliffe walked out of Maybury Hall into the weak sunshine. Mike escorted him past the guards on the gate. 'Where are you parked?'

'Just round the corner.'

Once they were out of the gates Ratcliffe turned to him. 'Your group captain,' he said to Mike, 'is he a patriot?'

'Yes,' said Mike, 'a good one.'

Allison was sketching the machine's innards from memory. Rachel looked over her shoulder and made the occasional suggestion.

'The weapon stick,' said Rachel as Allison's pencil started marking out the curve of the complicated gimble joint, 'what do you think?'

'If it's not a light-maser I don't have any viable ideas. One thing, though,' she flipped pages to show another sketch, 'this seemed to be the control line, but…'

'It wasn't electrical wiring,' finished Rachel. 'No, it was something like extruded glass, a very pure glass fibre.'

Concepts formed in Rachel's mind: she envisaged bursts of coherent light modulated to carry digital signals down a net of pure glass fibre... The image broke up. I must be getting tired,' she said. 'I had an idea and then it just went out of my mind.' She shrugged and looked at the sketch again. 'We need to get it to a decent biology lab.'

'And a half decent biologist,' said Allison. 'You think it's extra-terrestrial, don't you?'

Rachel nodded. 'The question is how much do we tell the group captain?'

'Ah,' said Allison archly, 'you're the chief scientific adviser; it's your decision.'

'Before I tell him anything I want to catch up with the Doctor.'

'You think he knows something?'

'Yes,' said Rachel, and she suddenly remembered the Doctor's eyes, 'and considerably more than he's telling us.'

'I thought you'd been here before,' said Ace as she recognized a pub they had passed before. The Doctor ignored her, peering intently over the steering wheel.

'There!' he cried, and swung the van down a side street into Coal Hill Road. A minute later they pulled up alongside Coal Hill School. Ace grabbed her tape deck and jumped out, following the Doctor towards the gate.

'Why are we here?' she asked.

'This is where Rachel detected the primary source of the transmissions. Come on.'

Transmission of what? thought Ace as she hurried after the Doctor.

The inside of the school was all cream-coloured brick and bright, crude pictures. Ace felt a shock of recognition: it wasn't so different from the concrete palace in Perivale where she had spent five years serving out her adolescence – the same notice-board and the same deserted feeling once the kids had gone home. But there were differences. Murals decorated walls in Ace's school of the 1980s: there were scenes from Africa and India, notices for Ramadan, Passover, Caribbean nights, and concerts by the school reggae ensemble.

I bet they don't teach sociology here, she thought, and suddenly she was nostalgic for the future. I hated school, didn't I? she continued. It loomed up behind her, summer-term light glinting off glass set in concrete as she sat on the wall with Manisha, Judy and Claire. They were laughing and talking about music and what they wanted from life. They must have been fourteen because Ace remembered the way Manisha's long black hair floated in the breeze, before she lost it in the fire. No! She wasn't going to remember that – it hasn't even happened yet. It's still twenty years in the future.

A man was pinning notices onto a board. He turned as the Doctor and Ace approached. He had a wide, bland face and watery grey eyes.

'Good evening,' he said, 'and you must be…?'

'The Doctor. And you?'

'I'm the headmaster.' A flicker of puzzlement washed across his face. 'Doctor, eh? You're a bit overqualified for the position, but if you'd like to leave your particulars and references.'

'References?'

'You are here for the position as school caretaker?'

'We're here for a quite different reason.'

'Oh.' The headmaster stepped back slightly. 'What can I do for you then?'

'I'd like to have a quick look round your school, if you don't mind?'

The headmaster shook his head. 'I'm afraid that's out of the question.'

'We have reason to believe that there is a great evil at work somewhere in this school.'

That was a convincing line, thought Ace.

The headmaster chuckled. 'You'll have to be a bit more specific, Doctor.' The chuckle broke off, there was a pause and then: 'But I don't think it would do any harm if you were to have just a quick look round.'

'Thank you,' said the Doctor.

'My pleasure,' said the headmaster.

Rachel watched as Mike reported the status of the units to Gilmore. More detector vans were being hurriedly rigged by artificers and deployed in central and east London.

'Are the anti-tank rockets being issued?' asked Gilmore.

Mike checked his clipboard. 'They're being taken direct to the positions; the fire teams can pick them up there. I packed Kaufman off in a Land-Rover with half a dozen.'

'Where's he taking them?' asked Rachel.

'Coal Hill School,' said Mike.

'On his own?'

'Tell him to sit tight when he gets there,' said Gilmore. 'Any reports on the Doctor's whereabouts?'

Mike told them that Red Four, the van that the Doctor had borrowed, had been seen in the Coal Hill area.

'They must be making for the school,' said Gilmore. 'We'd better get down there ourselves.'

'What about the machine at Foreman's Yard?' asked Rachel.

Mike turned to her and smiled. 'Don't worry, it's under guard: it's safe.'

The two guards at Foreman's Yard were unaware of anything amiss until the pickaxe handles crashed down on their skulls. Both men toppled bonelessly to the ground and lay still. Their attackers, two men in anonymous workmen's jackets, grinned at each other – they enjoyed violence.

A flatbed truck backed into the yard, and more men in jackets jumped out. They moved deliberately towards the ruined Dalek.

Their leader gave directions and, clustering around the Dalek, the men began to haul it towards the truck.

'Get a move on,' called Ratcliffe. 'We haven't got all day.'

Ace and the Doctor stopped at the top of the stairwell. 'You were expecting these Daleks, weren't you?' asked Ace.

The Doctor swiftly opened a door to a classroom and

entered. The sweet welcoming smell of a chemistry lab met Ace as she followed the Doctor inside. Her eyes shopped quickly around the glass cabinets, looking for anything that might be useful.

'The Daleks are following me,' he paused, considering. 'They must have traced this time-space location from records they captured during their occupation of the Earth in the 22nd century.' He smiled. 'The amount of effort expended must have been incredible.' He opened a window and carefully leaned out.

'I wouldn't be so pleased if I had a bunch of Daleks on my case,' remarked Ace, dumping her tape deck on one of the benches.

'You can always judge a man by the quality of his enemies.' The Doctor called her over to the window. 'Have a look at this.' Ace leaned out of the window and looked down. 'What do you make of that?' he asked.

'It's a playground.'

'The burn marks, Ace. See them?'

Ace looked again.

'Well?'

Ace considered. 'Landing pattern of some kind of spacecraft, ain't it?'

'Very good,' the Doctor commended in his best genial teacher manner.

Thoughts occurred to Ace, disturbing thoughts. 'But this is Earth, 1963. Someone would have noticed – I'd have heard about it.'

'Do you remember the Nestene invasion?'

'Eh?'

'The Zygon gambit with the Loch Ness monster; the

Yetis in the Underground?'

'The what?'

'Your species has an amazing capacity for self-deception matched only by its ingenuity when trying to destroy itself.'

'You don't have to sound so smug about it.'

More things occurred to Ace as they left the chemistry lab. 'If the Daleks are following you, what are they after?'

The Doctor paused a moment in the corridor. 'When I was here before I left something behind. It musn't fall into the wrong hands.'

'You mean the Hand of Omega.'

'Yes.'

'What is the Hand of Omega?'

'Something very dangerous,' said the Doctor. He started down the stairwell.

George Ratcliffe watched as his men put the tarpaulin-shrouded mass down in the lumber storage area. He dismissed the men, instructing them to be ready when he called on them. Then, pulling aside a heavy sliding door, he walked into a dimly lit office. Against one wall lights pulsed on a console, in front of which sat a figure in shadow.

'Report.' Its voice was harsh and mechanical.

'My men have recovered the machine. The Doctor is co-operating with the military.'

'That is to be expected. I must be informed of his movements.'

'Yes. We have certain contacts; I shall see that he is followed,' Ratcliffe replied evenly. Then he voiced his concern. 'That Dalek machine?'

'Yes?'

Ratcliffe spoke carefully: 'I would like to know exactly what it is.' He waited – this master could be difficult to work with.

'A machine, a tool, nothing more.'

Ace watched as the Doctor nosed around the ground floor. 'What are we looking for?'

'Whoever it was that landed their spaceship in the playground.'

Ace considered this. 'And they are?'

'More Daleks.'

'Oh good, I thought it might be something nasty.'

The Doctor motioned towards a heavy iron door. 'The cellar,' he said, 'it should be down there.'

'Why the cellar?' asked Ace apprehensively.

'Good place to put things, cellars.' He opened the door to reveal a flight of wrought-iron steps leading down into a well of darkness.

'I wish I had some more nitro-nine,' said Ace as she followed the Doctor down.

'So do I,' he agreed.

Ace glanced round as her eyes adjusted to the gloom, but what she could see didn't look any better. 'What do you expect to find down here?'

'The unknown.'

'Oh,' said Ace. Reaching over her shoulder she drew a baseball bat out of her rucksack. The bat was made of plastic over rubber on an aluminium core and painted silver: it wasn't much of a weapon, but it made her feel better. 'Isn't this a bit dangerous then?'

'Probably,' agreed the Doctor, 'but if I knew what was down here, I wouldn't have to look.'

The stairs twisted down into an old boiler room. Ace could see through gaps in the surrounding wall tangles of piping and a huge boiler painted a flaking cream. An alien machine lay in a cleared space, backed against the grimy wall. It consisted of a small dais with two upright cabinets with severe alien lines on either side.

Ace immediately jumped onto the dais. 'This is some severe technology,' she said gleefully.

The Doctor pulled her off the dais and opened the nearest cabinet. Inside, matt black boxes nested in fibre optic connections.

'Very elegant, very advanced – flux circuit elements.'

'What does it do?'

'It's a transmat – a matter transmitter – but transmitting from where?' He carefully traced the connections to the power regulator.

Ace realized she could hear a low threshold hum. She looked around the cellar for its source before focusing suspiciously on the dais. Its surface was definitely beginning to glow.

'Professor?'

'Range of about three hundred kilometres.'

The glow began to elongate upwards, forming a jelly mould shape one and a half metres high. Colours shot across its surface.

'Professor,' Ace called warily, 'something is activating the transmat.'

'Yes, very likely,' mused the Doctor as he easily

located the control node. 'It has a remote activator.' He turned sharply to Ace. 'What?'

Ace nodded at the dais. The jelly mould shape had begun to fill up with shapes, and for a moment she saw something moving weakly among a cradle of translucent filaments.

'You're right!' cried the Doctor. 'Something is beginning to come through.' He plunged back into the transmat's circuits.

Ace hefted her baseball bat uneasily, watching as the shape solidified one layer at a time. In a moment the outer shell flowed together like coalescing globules of mercury.

'It's another Dalek,' said Ace.

'Excellent,' said the Doctor.

The casing was almost fully formed. It was pale cream with gold trimmings, different from the one the Doctor had blown up earlier. Different, wondered Ace, how different? 'Will this one be friendly?' she asked.

The Doctor looked surprised. 'I sincerely doubt that.' He quickly rigged two cables together. 'Now if I can just cause the receiver to dephase at the critical point…'

The hum oscillated out of the range of human hearing. Ace realized that the climax was approaching – the Dalek was slowly becoming solid – so she raised her baseball bat. 'Doctor!' Ace cried.

The Doctor twisted something inside the machine. 'Get down,' he shouted and pulled Ace away and onto the ground.

The transmat howled as splinters of light arced from the dais. There was a vast grinding sound and the air filled with a blizzard of Dalek fragments.

Ace looked up to find herself staring at the twisted end of an eyestick. It was coloured gold and stared blindly back. She quickly got up and bent to examine the transmat. Whisps of dust whirled around in the decaying transmission field before they too settled on the surface of the dais.

'The controls have gone dead,' she told the Doctor.

'The misphase must have caused an overload.'

'What did you do to it?'

'I persuaded one half of the Dalek to materialize where the other half was materializing. They both tried to coexist at the same points and the resultant reaction destroyed them.' He made an expansive gesture with his arms and then patted the top of one of the cabinets. 'Dangerous things, transmats.'

'So no more Daleks can be transported through here.'

'Well,' the Doctor said cautiously, 'we seem to have slowed them down a bit, at least until the operator can repair the system.'

The word operator bounced about at the back of Ace's mind for a moment. Hold on, she thought. 'The operator?'

'The Daleks usually leave an operator on station to deal with any malfunction.'

A very bad scenario started to occur to Ace. 'And that would be another Dalek?'

'Yes,' said the Doctor.

There was a wrenching crash from behind the supporting wall.

I have a bad feeling about this, thought Ace as she

and the Doctor turned towards the sound. A cream and gold Dalek was pulling away from the heating system's pipes. It must have been there all the time – I looked right at it and ignored it, Ace berated herself. She had a sick certainty that it wasn't going to be easy to ignore in about ten seconds. Ace shifted her grip on the bat and wondered if the Dalek had any weaknesses. She wasn't too upset when the Doctor yelled at her to run for it.

'Stay where you are,' shrieked the Dalek. 'Do not move.'

Ace made the stairs marginally ahead of the Doctor, but only because she vaulted the handrail. Bouncing off the rail as she turned the corner, Ace saw a rectangle of light above – the doorway.

Behind her there was a crash: the Dalek screamed orders, and somebody – the Doctor? – cursed in a language that had more vowel sounds than consonants. She virtually dived through the doorway, and collided with somebody on the other side.

'Sorry,' she said stupidly as she recognized the headmaster. She was about to warn him about the Dalek when his knee hit her midriff and sent her winded to the floor.

Tripping on the stairs caused the Doctor to remember some very obscure Gallifreyan colloquialism. He ignored the Dalek's orders and instead concentrated on getting up the stairs. He recognized it as a low caste warrior – and they rarely said anything interesting.

A whine behind him indicated that a Dalek motivator was powering up to design limits. The Doctor turned to see the Dalek lift easily on a band of colour and follow him up the stairs. So that's how they do it, he thought, and charged up the steps to safety. He was just wondering why the Dalek hadn't opened fire when the door slammed in his face.

The headmaster was throwing the last bolt of the door when he was hit in the stomach by fifty kilograms of enraged teenager. As the headmaster toppled gasping to the ground, Ace frantically jerked the bolts free and opened the iron door. The Doctor fell out, back first, and Ace caught a glimpse of cream and gold before she threw the door closed and slammed home the bolts.

'What's the matter with him?' asked the Doctor, looking at the prone headmaster.

'Stomach ache.'

The Doctor grabbed the headmaster's arm and started to drag him away from the doorway. 'Give me a hand.'

Ace was outraged. 'Professor! He tried to lock you in.'

'Ace,' the Doctor said sternly. Ace took the other arm and together they pulled the man clear. The Doctor checked behind the man's ear and exposed a dull red implant grafted into the skin. Ace looked at the Doctor – his face was grim but not surprised – then they both ran out of the school. As they reached the exit a vast bang echoed down the corridor.

'That was the door,' said the Doctor as they quickly ran across the playground.

A military Land-Rover was parked outside. The portly uniformed man beside it with sergeant's stripes looked bemused as Ace and the Doctor bore down on him. He opened his mouth to speak.

'What are you doing here?' demanded the Doctor. The sergeant's mouth closed and then opened again. 'Never mind. Get this vehicle out of here.'

'I was ordered to deliver the ATRs to this position, sir,' he said defensively.

The Doctor's eyes snapped round to the truck, 'ATRs – anti-tank rockets?'

'Yes, sir.'

'Wicked,' said Ace, ignoring another stern look from the Doctor, 'we can use them against the Da…'

'No,' said the Doctor. 'Violence isn't the answer to everything.' He turned to the sergeant. 'You'll have to pull back.'

'My orders were to stay in this position,' the man said stubbornly.

'This particular position,' the Doctor said evenly, 'is about to become somewhat untenable when that Dalek catches up with us.'

'Except it hasn't come out yet,' Ace pointed out somewhat snidely.

'I wonder why not?'

Ace noticed that the sergeant's eyes were getting a bit glazed. 'Maybe it went back to fix the transmat?' she suggested.

'Probably,' agreed the Doctor.

There was a short pause.

'Don't just stand there,' said the Doctor sharply to the sergeant. 'Break out the rockets.' The sergeant quickly cracked open a crate and pulled out a bulky metal launcher. He seemed reluctant to hand it over. 'What's your name, sergeant?' barked the Doctor.

'Kaufman.'

'Sir!' snapped the Doctor.

'Quartermaster-Sergeant Kaufman, sir!' He saluted smartly as the Doctor relieved him of the rocket launcher. 'To get it ready, sir,' he started helpfully, 'you...'

The Doctor snapped the sights upright, pulled the trigger guard into position, released the firing restraint pin and checked the battery power. Kaufman mutely handed over a rocket which the Doctor slotted into the correct position before re-engaging the safety. He gave the assembled weapon to Ace.

Kaufman still made the Doctor sign for it before they left. 'Sorry, sir, regulations,' he explained.

'We're not after the Dalek,' explained the Doctor, 'we're after the transmat.' He flattened himself to the wall one side of the entrance, motioning to Ace to take the position opposite. He carefully checked inside and then burst through the doors; Ace followed, rocket launcher ready for use.

The hallway was deserted.

'Won't the Dalek try to stop us?'

'Quite possibly,' he warned. 'Stay close behind me,'

That's clever, thought Ace, seeing as I'm the one carrying the weapon. She was just suggesting that the Dalek must have gone back down into the cellar when a bolt of energy slashed past her and blew a cast iron radiator off the wall.

They quickly hid behind a table that the Doctor had upended. Wisps of smoke rose from a charred hole in one of the classroom doors.

Things then happened very fast. The Dalek came through the door, smashing it into toothpicks, and fired. A trophy cabinet to Ace's left burst in a shower of glass, the splinters bouncing off the walls.

Ace raised the launcher to her shoulder, lined up the sights as best she could, and pulled the trigger. There was a blast of heat behind her and a lot of smoke.

The rocket had barely started to accelerate when it struck the grille just below the Dalek's eyestalk, but it was going fast enough to detonate. Superheated gases punched a hole in the Dalek's polycarbide casing, ripped through the delicate circuits and soft organic parts, and blew them out of the back in a spray of shattered armour.

'Ace,' she breathed softly.

'You destroyed it.'

'I aimed at the eyepiece.'

The Doctor looked at her with something close to despair.

There was a clatter of army boots in the hallway. Mike was shouting orders as he came round the corner. 'Keep sharp, watch your back, watch your...' His voice wound down as he faced Ace, the Doctor and an obviously dead Dalek. 'Doctor, Ace.' He paused, eyeing the Dalek. 'Any more?'

'No,' said the Doctor.

Mike, ordered a soldier back to fetch the group captain. Then he noticed the rocket launcher that Ace was carrying. 'Did you do that?'

Ace waved smoke away from her face and nodded.

'Makes a lot of smoke, doesn't it?' She handed over the weapon – it was getting heavy. Mike gave her a strange look, almost like awe, as he took it.

The Doctor considered his next move, watching as the group captain, Professor Jensen and her assistant, Miss Williams, entered the corridor. They represented a flaw, a deviation from the plan, as did the Dalek at Foreman's Yard.

Gilmore looked coldly at the smoking Dalek. 'You destroyed it, good.'

Anger coursed through the Doctor, shocking and unexpected in its intensity. 'It is not good. Nothing about this is good. I have made a grave error of judgement.'

The plan was becoming blurred around the edges, and within that uncertainty people were beginning to die. 'I'm beginning to wish I'd never started this,' he said softly to himself.

He looked at the others, their faces filled with expectation, and he wondered if he was going to get them killed. He fixed Gilmore with his eyes. 'Group Captain, I must ask you to evacuate the immediate area.'

'That's an absurd idea,' snapped Gilmore.

'Why, Doctor?' Rachel interjected quickly, forestalling any dismissal by Gilmore.

'I have reason, reasons,' he corrected, 'to believe that a major Dalek task-force could soon be operating in this area.'

'Great,' said Allison.

'And where,' demanded Gilmore, 'will this task-force arrive from?'

'One certainly is already in place, hidden somewhere in this vicinity.'

Now there is a comforting thought, said a voice in Rachel's head.

'The other,' continued the Doctor, 'probably from a timeship in geostationary orbit.'

How easily he says these things, as if they were commonplace, thought Rachel.

'Come on, Doctor,' Gilmore said stubbornly, 'be reasonable.'

But the Doctor was not reasonable. 'Do you dispute the non-terrestrial nature of the Daleks? Examine this,' he gestured angrily at the remains, 'or better still ask your scientific adviser.'

Gilmore turned on her. 'Well, Professor Jensen?'

Rachel knew Gilmore wasn't going to like her reply. 'The Doctor is right. It's alien.'

Gilmore looked betrayed. 'You're positive?'

'Yes.'

The group captain thought about it. 'Professor, a word please.' He drew Rachel away from the others. 'This Doctor chappie, do you trust him?'

'He knows what he is talking about and considerably more, than he is telling us. I think we should go along with him for now.'

'And after?'

Rachel shrugged. 'We could ask for an explanation.'

'We might,' said Gilmore, and there was steel in his tone, 'do a bit more than ask.' He turned back to the Doctor. 'I'll have to get a decision from my superiors.'

'When?' asked the Doctor.

'I should get a decision either way by tomorrow morning. I'll see you all then.' And with that he strode out.

'Can you look after Ace for me?' the Doctor asked Rachel.

'Of course.' As he was turning to leave she ventured: 'Doctor, I have questions I would like answered.'

'So have I,' said the Doctor. 'I'll return in the morning.'

Ace ran up to him. 'Doctor, where are you going?'

'I have to bury the past.'

'I'm coming with you.'

He shook his head. 'It's not your past, Ace. You haven't been born yet.' He plucked the baseball bat from her rucksack. 'I'll take that.' Settling it under his arm he left.

Rachel took Ace's hand and looked into her eyes. 'What did he mean, haven't been born yet?'

Ace smiled but said nothing.

The workshop was a vast globe one kilometre across, its walls studded with sensors. Cables as thick as corridors snaked uneasily around its vertical circumference. People worked amid this vast technology, insect-like in protective garments.

In the exact centre hung a radiance like a tiny sun, pulsing unevenly to its own secret rhythms.

The Triumvirate met in a gallery high in the upper hemisphere. Of these three Gallifreyans who would reshape their world, two were to become great legends; the other would vanish altogether from history.

Omega turned away from the gallery window. He was a huge man with wide shoulders and muscular arms, a definite drift from the regenerative norm. Some Gallifreyans, however, said his present incarnation was a throwback, a genetic memory from the dark time. He opened his arms like some barbarian king and grinned at Rassilon.

'Well,' he said, 'we have succeeded.'

'In what, Omega,' Rassilon said quietly, 'have we succeeded?'

'Why, the key to time,' Omega said unconcernedly. 'You as much as any of us have made this instrument possible.' He turned to the third person in the room. 'Is this not true?'

'It is,' said the other.

Disquiet was in Rassilon's pale eyes. 'And what shall we do with this power once we have it?'

'Why, cousin, we shall become transtemporal, free of the tyranny of moment following moment.' Omega thumped his chest. 'We shall become the Lords of Time.'

'Let us hope,' Rassilon said evenly, 'that we are worthy of such stewardship. Time imposes order on events; without order there is no balance, all is chaos.'

'Then we shall impose order...'

'I forbid it,' the other said suddenly.

'I was merely explaining...'

'Remember the Minyans,' said the other.

'But we know so much more, we have learnt from our mistakes,' protested Omega, but he met the other's eyes and became silent.

'We have obviously learnt nothing; we shall carry that stain forever.' He moved to the balcony and stared out at the device that burned in the chamber beyond.

'Whatever other chains we break.'

Rassilon and Omega joined him at the window.

'Is it not a magnificent achievement?' said Omega.

'Yes, it is that,' conceded Rassilon, 'a fantastic device.'

'Or a terrible weapon,' said the other.

4

SATURDAY, 02:17

The Doctor walked alone in the dark city down near the docks. How many times have I walked here, in this sprawling maze of streets and people? he thought.

Do they have fogs in London in 1963? He couldn't remember – there were so many details, so many worlds. Such a vast glittering universe, and yet it is always here.

This planet.

Its children will be flung out into the stars, to conquer, to fight and die on alien planets. Indomitable, fantastic, brilliant and yet so cruel, petty and selfish.

And it is always here that the final choices are made.

The Doctor watched awhile as a crane unloaded crates from a ship. A cold wind flicked scraps of paper along the street. He could see stars through a rent in the clouds.

'Don't you think you could get along without me,' he said softly into the night, 'just for a little while.'

Only the wind answered.

The Doctor smelt the tea on the breeze. He sighed once and walked upwind.

'Can I help you?' asked John.

The tea-stall stood in a pool of light next to a warehouse. Hammering sounds came intermittently from the nearby docks, and occasionally the sound of a barge's horn would float up from the river.

The small white man with the umbrella and hat paused to look at the tariff.

'A mug of tea, please,' he said.

John poured a mug of black tea from the urn. 'Cold night tonight,' he said, adding milk.

'Yes, it is,' said the man, cupping the mug in his hands. 'Bitter, very bitter.'

'Sugar?'

'Ah,' said the man, 'a decision.' He sighed and sipped his tea. 'Would it make any difference?'

John looked at the man to see if he was joking or something. 'It would make your tea sweet,' he said after a pause.

The man gave a wan smile. 'But beyond the confines of my taste-buds, would it make any difference.'

'Not really.'

'But…' The man leaned forward conspiratorially, eyes glittering. They were compelling eyes.

'But what?' asked John, suddenly anxious to know.

'But what if I could control everybody's taste-buds?' He made a broad, sweeping gesture. 'What if I decided that no one would take sugar? That would make a difference, wouldn't it, to the people who sell sugar and those that cut cane…'

John remembered his father, hands bleeding as he hacked at the bright green stalks under a cobalt sky. 'My father,' said John, 'he was a cane-cutter.'

'Exactly. If no one used sugar then your father wouldn't have been a cane-cutter.'

'If this sugar thing had never started,' said John, 'my great grandfather wouldn't have been kidnapped, chained up and sold in the first place. I'd be an African.' The idea was strangely comforting to John.

'See,' said the man, 'every large decision creates ripples, like a truck dropped in a river. The ripples can merge, rebound off the banks in unforeseeable ways.' He looked suddenly tired. 'The heavier the decision, the greater the waves and the more uncertain the consequence.'

John shrugged. 'Life's like that,' he said. 'Best thing is just to get on with it.'

Professor Rachel Jensen lay asleep in her bed at the boarding house run by Mike's mother on Ashton Road. After the Doctor and Gilmore had left them, they had returned here for supper before retiring. Now Rachel dreamed of her childhood in Golders Green.

She was sitting beside her mother in the synagogue. Bright sunlight streamed in through high windows, but the spaces behind the benches were in deep shadow. Rachel was sure something was moving in those dark spaces. She forced herself to look back at Rabbi Goldsmith who was reading from the Talmud.

Only he wasn't there. Instead an intense little man in a pale jacket was speaking, punctuating his phrases by stabbing at the air with a red-handled umbrella. Rachel knew he was saying something of great importance, only strain as hard as she might she could not make out his words.

All the time, squat evil shapes materialized in the

shadows – shapes with smooth domes and gritty voices.

Across the landing from Rachel, Ace twisted in the strange bed, tangling herself in the crisp cotton sheets. In her sleep, fragmentary images flashed across her eyes like a badly edited rock video. She dreamed of the time when her name was Dorothy.

Dorothy was fourteen, facing the burnt-out shell of Manisha's house. The blaring sound of fire sirens wound about her head counterpointed by a dry BBC voice: 'Petrol was poured through the letter box and set on fire: the house was gutted in minutes. Two members of the family managed to escape, but the rest, including the mother, father and three young children, were killed. The police say they are considering the possibility of a racial motive. This is the fourth such incident in Perivale in the last six months. Community leaders…'

Then Dorothy stood at the end of a hospital bed: she could smell vomit overlaid by disinfectant. Nearby, old wrinkled women groaned and muttered complaints. A bunch of grapes hung pathetically in her hand. She stared at Manisha's face, noticing the way the skin had bubbled on her cheeks and the raw meat under dressings on her scalp.

Months later Dorothy watched as her friend's eyes turned lacklustre and dead. She waved goodbye as Manisha left Perivale – left Dorothy – to stay with relatives in Birmingham. Manisha had gone for good.

It was Dorothy who stared at the burnt house, the burnt face, the burnt life, the racist graffiti. And it was Dorothy who stared at the words 'Pakis out' on the wall of the playground.

It was Ace who blew away the wall with two and a half kilograms of nitro-nine.

Fireball in the darkness.

Fire fighting fire.

5

SATURDAY, 06:26

Martin gave the screwdriver a final twist and straightened up. He tugged the handle to make sure the brass fitted snugly against the fine oak of the coffin: his back gave a twinge and he rubbed it idly while checking his handiwork. Martin was in the middle of rubbing down the surface finish when he heard a click behind him.

The sound echoed in the silent room.

Martin's palms suddenly became damp.

Another click, like a rifle bolt being slammed closed.

Martin slowly turned to face the noise.

The casket was almost seven feet long, constructed of metal which was pitted and dirty with age. It seemed to Martin to be, well, somehow expectant.

Unnerved, Martin moved closer. He saw that two of the lid's catches were open. He reached out cautiously to close the nearest – cold burned his fingertips and he snatched back his hand. The top layer of skin had been torn from the pads of his fingers.

Another catch sprang open, this time in front of his eyes. Sweating, Martin backed away from the casket. He had the horrible idea that whatever was in the casket was alive and wanted to get out. He backed into something and whirled, a scream choking off in his throat.

A man in a pale jacket stood there, an umbrella in one hand and a bottle of milk in the other. 'Good morning,' the man said pleasantly. 'I believe this belongs to you.' He held up the bottle.

Not trusting his voice, Martin nodded and took the bottle, still conscious of the tangible presence of the casket behind him.

'The door was open,' explained the man, 'so I thought I'd just pop in and collect my casket.'

'Ah well,' said Martin, 'I'm afraid the governor has yet to arrive and I really can't let you…' His voice trailed off; the man smiled pleasantly at him. 'Which, ah, casket would this be?'

The man nodded towards the metal casket behind Martin.

'I see,' said Martin. 'Well, if you could just wait until the governor arrives, I'm sure…'

'That would be perfectly all right ,' said the man.

Martin suddenly felt immensely relieved. 'Good, splendid, Mister…?'

'Doctor.'

'Doctor…?' Martin asked hopefully.

'If I might have just a few moments alone?'

'Of course, of course. I'll just leave you with your…'

'Thank you.'

'I'll be just next door if you require anything,' said Martin as he made a hasty exit.

It was there: the presence, the aura as distinctive as a genetic pattern, sharp as a blade. Perception was difficult in this strange cold environment with its slabs of molecules that moved so slowly, its alien auras that flickered so weakly around it. The environment was so unlike the vast hot spaces it loved or the powerful minds of its creators.

Deep in its most fundamental programming, where rapidly shifting fields of energy interacted, it quivered in anticipation of the data it would receive. Instructions would come: instructions meant purpose; purpose meant function; function meant life!

The Doctor faced the casket. 'Open,' he said.

The remaining buckles snapped open with the sound of gunshots. The seals cracked apart and light spilled through the rapidly widening gap as the lid pulled itself up and back. A deep thrumming filled the room.

The Doctor pulled the baseball bat from concealment. 'Now,' he said, holding it carefully over the yawning casket, 'let's see what you can make of this.' He let go of the bat and watched as it slowly descended into the blazing white heart of the radiance.

Somebody was knocking on her door.

Ace sat up, struggling to untangle her legs from the sheets.

'Come in.'

Mike stuck his head round the door.

'Good morning,' he said.

Ace could smell bacon sandwich.

'Good morning,' said Ace. Carefully holding the blanket above chest level, she fumbled in her rucksack for a clean T-shirt.

Mike pushed open the door and stepped into the room. His eyes never left her as he took a bite from the bacon sandwich in his right hand. Ace wondered what he was staring at.

You know what he is staring at, said a voice in her head.

Ace hiked up the blanket a bit more.

'Did you make a sandwich for me?'

Mike moved closer.

'What do you want?' he said. 'Breakfast in bed?'

'Why not? Isn't this a bed and breakfast?'

He was standing by the bed now, looking down at her. There was a sudden intensity in his eyes. Ace sensed that he wanted to say something.

Mike offered her the bacon sandwich instead.

'Thanks,' she said.

Her hand touched his as she took the sandwich; his skin was warm and rough. Ace took a bite of the sandwich and offered it back to him. Mike shook his head.

'Keep it,' he said. 'I have to be off.'

'Where are you going?'

Mike turned at the doorway. 'I have to check some things at the Association.'

'Oh,' said Ace, not really interested.

Mike smiled again and said goodbye. Ace watched him go, thoughtfully munching on the sandwich. She couldn't understand just why she was interested in him; he wasn't that good looking, except maybe for his face.

She suddenly realized that fat had dripped onto one of the blankets; she wondered whether Mrs Smith would notice.

The device played with the toy. Insinuating parts of itself into the aluminium core, it played with the lattice of atoms, arranging them into convoluted patterns. As careful as a watchmaker, as gleeful as a three-year-old, the device stripped away the polymer chains of the covering and then relaid them in interesting new ways. Within moments the baseball bat became a room-temperature superconductor. Then, drawing on the latent heat in the surrounding atmosphere, the device poured energy into the bat. The ambient temperature in the room fell by one degree centigrade; a wafer-thin layer of ice formed on the casket's skin.

'Come on,' said the Doctor, 'give it up.'

The casket spat out the baseball bat. The Doctor snatched it out of the air and twirled it a bit before examining it.

'Good boy,' he commended. 'Now close.'

The lid closed with a whumph! of seals. The Doctor walked to the door and pulled it open. 'All right,' he said, 'follow me.'

Without any fuss or sound the casket levitated and floated after him.

In the corridor Martin was on the telephone.

'Gov'nor, somebody's come to collect that big casket. Yes… the Doctor. One thing, I thought you said he was an old geezer with white hair.'

The Doctor walked past him and doffed his hat.

'Goodbye, Doctor,' said Martin. 'What about your…'

The casket floated past him with nothing at all holding it up. Martin took one long look and fainted.

6

SATURDAY, 07:31

The Reverend Parkinson could feel the crunch of gravel under his feet, and smell the mown grass of the graveyard and the sharp tang of newly turned earth and wet leaves. Over the distant rumble of traffic he could hear the morning birds singing. All these were familiar gifts from God, compensations for having his sight taken away in the mud at Verdun.

He had been a captain, one of the many Oxford graduates who enlisted in 1914. They were the cream of a generation: winning battles on the playing fields of Eton; dying amid mud, spilled guts and mustard gas.

In some nameless dressing station, as he twisted and cried in a rough cot, he had been called to God. The vast compassion of the Creator pressed him down into peace and stillness.

Parkinson could feel that stillness now as he walked with an arm through one of the Doctor's. The Doctor always conjured a sense of quiet when he was near, like the calm at the eye of a storm.

'It's very good of you,' said the Doctor, 'to do this at such short notice.'

'Nonsense, my dear Doctor,' Parkinson answered. 'The grave has been ready for a month. Mr Stevens, the gravedigger, was most upset.'

'I had to leave suddenly,' explained the Doctor.

'Forgive me for saying this, but it seems to me that your voice has changed somewhat since we last met.' And it was true. Parkinson had hardlly recognized the voice that morning – a trace of Scottish, perhaps? Parkinson heard the Doctor chuckle softly.

'Oh, I have changed,' he said, 'several times.'

Parkinson felt rather then heard the coffin being laid over the grave.

'I must say,' he commented, 'your pall-bearers are very quiet, silent as ghosts really.'

Ratcliffe started when the telephone rang. With one eye on the figure in the shadows he picked up the receiver. 'Good, stay with the Doctor and call me back... yours is not to reason why, just to follow orders... Good... Get on with it.' He slapped down the telephone and turned to the figure.

'My man has found it,' he said with some satisfaction.

'Yes,' said the figure, 'but my enemies have found your man.'

In a telephone box by the gates of the cemetery, Mike Smith put down the telephone and stepped out into the weak sunshine. Then, checking that no one was looking, he slipped through the gates and into the graveyard. He had seen the Doctor and the vicar heading behind the church that stood at the centre of the cemetery, so he increased his pace to catch up. He wanted to see if the coffin was still floating in that disturbing way. Miraculous things were happening around this strange

Doctor, things that the Association should know about. Besides, he owed Ratcliffe favours.

Suddenly he was choking, an arm tight around his throat, fabric rough on his cheek. A voice whispered in his ear: 'What is the location of the renegade Dalek base?'

Mike grabbed at the arm, trying to prise it loose, but the pressure only got worse. 'Get off me,' he gasped. 'I'll break your legs.'

The man repeated the question, the choking grip emphasizing his advantage.

Mike didn't know what the man was talking about. He tried to tell the man this, but spots of light were blurring his eyes.

'You are an agent of the renegade Daleks,' said the man.

What? thought Mike. He went limp. 'I work for Mr Ratcliffe, the Association.' With a sudden burst of energy he twisted in the man's grip, breaking the hold on his throat, and pulled his adversary's arm back and up. The man grunted as Mike applied an arm lock, then seized a handful of white hair and savagely pulled back his head. Mike was shocked to discover that his attacker was old, maybe in his fifties.

'Who do you work for?'

But the man gazed stupidly past Mike's face; his old body tensed and jerked like a puppet. A low moan escaped his lips. With a shock Mike recognized him as the headmaster of Coal Hill School. The body went limp and slid out of Mike's hands, slumping boneless and dead to the ground.

Mike recoiled, breathing hard. He looked wildly about. No one was in sight; no one had seen. He ran, leaving the headmaster among the maze of gravestones.

But he ran after the Doctor.

'Ashes to ashes, dust to dust,' intoned Parkinson and snapped his braille bible shut. He heard the Doctor reach over and then the rattle of dirt on the coffin lid. 'It's over,' he said after a respectful pause.

'No,' replied the Doctor, 'it's just starting.'

It was only as the Doctor led him away that Parkinson realized he didn't know whom he had just buried.

Mike watched the Doctor walk away, arm and arm with the vicar. He fixed the position of the grave in his mind, the better to report to Ratcliffe later.

Ratcliffe had told him he would see many strange things and he was right, as usual. He had always known things, secrets. When Mike was small, running wild on the bombsites, Ratcliffe had given him a bar of chocolate – a small bar with foreign words on the wrapper. 'It's from Germany,' Ratcliffe had explained.

'You been there?' Many returning soldiers had brought back things from overseas.

'No, Mike me lad,' said Ratcliffe, 'but I've got friends there.'

The chocolate had been rich and dark; Mike made it last a long time. As Mike grew up, Ratcliffe would talk to him. He told Mike about the world: how the bankers and communists were all in league together; how the government planned to ship in negroes from abroad to keep wages down and force decent white people out of their jobs.

Mike had absorbed it all.

Ratcliffe's pronouncements had of late become less general and more accurate. Last Saturday, Ratcliffe had caught him in Harry's Cafe. He had asked what Mike was doing in civvies. Mike had winked and told him it was a secret. Ratcliffe seemed to find that enormously funny, then he had leaned over the table and whispered in Mike's ear: 'There'll be a new American President by this evening.'

With that, he winked hugely and left.

That afternoon in Dallas, Kennedy's head jerked forward and then back.

'Secrets,' Ratcliffe had always said, 'are the key to everything.'

'Once we possess this Hand of Omega,' said Ratcliffe, 'what then?'

'We shall be on the brink of great power.'

'And our agreement?'

'You too shall share this power, if you have the stomach for it.'

Ratcliffe licked his suddenly dry lips. 'What do you mean?'

'There will be casualties, many deaths.'

Ratcliffe relaxed, shrugged and said: 'War is hell.'

Ace bit into a slice of toast.

The boarding house in Ashton Road was one of a row of jerry-built terraced houses that had survived the

Blitz. To the north the big concrete mistakes of post-war planning still gleamed hopefully over Hoxton. It was a dying community: children had vanished into the new towns out of London, leaving parents isolated. Doors were locked during the day now; mistrust showed in hard looks and muttered curses.

In the dining room of the house, the carpet had worn thin in places and the covers of the stuffed chairs were shiny at the seams from a thousand washes. A faded picture of Mr Smith in naval uniform hung on the wall: he had been lost with his ship in the freezing Arctic Sea while running weapons to the Russians in 1943.

Under that picture Mrs Smith laboured to keep her home spotless for the people who stayed there and for the stubborn pride of the bereaved. Everyday Mrs Smith would dust the knick-knacks from abroad that littered the mantelpiece with memories. She dusted the new television that Mike had bought but she never watched; she laid out breakfast places on the gate-legged table under the window.

At this table on that morning Rachel nibbled toast and remembered Turing. Ever since Turing had compared the human brain to eight pounds of cold porridge, Rachel had always thought about him at breakfast. She had also gone off porridge for good.

Across the table Allison read the paper, with studied intensity, her face unreadable. A war baby, thought Rachel, who had trouble understanding the way her assistant thought sometimes. I wonder what kind of world her generation will create, Aldous Huxley or George Orwell? She had a horrible suspicion that for an answer all she had to do was ask Ace: 'It's not your past, Ace,' the Doctor had said. 'You haven't been born yet.'

I must be getting old, thought Rachel, because I really don't want to know.

'The Professor said he'd be back by now,' Ace said suddenly.

'What was he up to, anyway?' asked Rachel.

'Working,' said the Doctor from the doorway, 'unlike some people.'

Mike was grinning over the Doctor's shoulder. 'Have a good sleep?'

"S OK,' said Ace. 'You're late.'

'I found him wandering the streets,' said Mike.

'I was not wandering,' the Doctor said testily. 'I was merely contemplating certain cartographical anomalies.'

Mrs Smith handed Mike a note.

Mike read it. 'Ladies and gentlemen,' he announced, 'if you don't mind I think the group captain is waiting for us.'

Ace sprang out of her seat. 'Great! something to do at last.'

'Ah,' said Mike. 'He specifically ordered that "the girl" should remain here.'

That did not go down well with Ace. She appealed to the Doctor, but he merely shrugged and pulled the baseball bat out of its hiding place in the umbrella.

'I brought you a present,' he said. He held up the bat and for a moment blue energy crackled about its tip.

Rachel recoiled. That wasn't static – static doesn't flow like that, she thought. That's another damned energy weapon. 'How did you do that?' she asked before she could stop herself.

'Higher technology,' the Doctor said airily, 'and no I can't tell you how.'

Rachel had to ask: 'Why not?'

'You're not ready for it – nobody on this planet is.'

There he goes again, Rachel thought.

Ace was protesting even as she took the bat. Rachel drew Allison out through the door.

Mike followed, but paused in the doorway. 'Sorry, kid,' he said to Ace. 'Work to be done. Back at six – have dinner ready.' He closed the door quickly behind him.

Ace said something loudly from the other side.

'Where did she learn words like that?' said Allison.

'She certainly has a colourful command of the English language,' agreed Rachel.

'No doubt about it,' said Mike, grinning, 'she isn't from Cambridge.' He ignored Allison's sour look and opened the front door. 'Come on, we can wait in the car.'

Ace struggled with her temper. 'Professor, you can't leave me here.' Her voice had a childish whine which even she noticed.

'Ace,' said the Doctor with exaggerated patience, 'I'm trying to persuade Gilmore to keep his men out of trouble. If I can't do that, a great number of needless deaths will occur.'

'You're up to something.'

'Yes.'

'Then I have to come with you.'

'No.'

'Who else is going to guard your back?'

'Will you obey me just this once? When I get back I'll explain everything.'

'Tell me now.'

'I don't have time.'

Grown-up against child again, thought Ace. Even with the Doctor it always comes down to that. But a nagging voice told her that this time she deserved it.

'I'll stay, if that's what you want.'

'Trust me,' said the Doctor. She did – all the way.

'Doctor?' she said as the Doctor opened the door.

He half turned. 'Yes?'

'You'd better explain when you get back, or…'

'Or?'

Ace lifted the baseball bat; blue light flickered briefly around it. 'Things could get nasty.' She smiled and as he closed the door she thought he smiled back. A chintz curtain swirled in the draft; seaman Smith stared down on her with faded eyes.

Ace wondered whether Mrs Smith had some nitrate fertilizer and some spare sugar. That was how she had started when she was twelve: a bag of nitrate fertilizer, a two-pound packet of sugar and some empty paint tins. The trick, she learned early on, was containment. The force of the blast comes from the rapidly expanding gases created by the reaction of the chemicals. With a crude explosive – 'sweetener' she had called her early stuff – the better the paint tin was sealed, the better the bang.

When she was fourteen she discovered the love of her life – nitroglycerine. With chemicals taken from the chemistry lab she synthesized her own, graduating to making nitrocellulose and then industrial grade gelignite.

One evening she hit upon nitro-nine, a forced recombination of the nitrate solution with a minimal organic stabilizer made up from shredded cornflake packets. Nitro-nine had awesome destructive powers – it was also very unstable.

But then, Ace figured, so was life.

Mike leaned on the steering wheel and stared gloomily after the Doctor. 'I wonder what he's up to?'

Rachel was trying unsuccessfully to find a comfortable position for her legs under the dashboard and wondering why she as chief scientific adviser rated only a Ford Prefect. 'Who knows?' she said flippantly. 'He has alien motives.'

Mike turned to her. 'Meaning?'

'Meaning, I don't think he's human.'

Mike's expression grew concerned. 'And Ace?'

'Oh, she's not an alien,' Rachel said slyly. 'You're all right there.'

The young man looked relieved. 'Good,' he said, quickly adding: 'I wouldn't want her to be foreign, would I?'

Rachel suppressed a laugh.

'Here comes the Doctor,' said Allison. 'Looks like he's carrying something.'

'Looks like a toolcase,' said Mike.

More magic, thought Rachel.

7

SATURDAY, 12:13

Ratcliffe started when a section of the wall slid noiselessly up into the ceiling to reveal a large flat screen. It took him a few moments to resolve the sharp grey lines and red blobs into a recognizable picture. It was like one of those hideous abstracts that decadent people thought of as art. Except, he realized, it was an aerial view of the immediate area. A green symbol flashed near the centre on what Ratcliffe was sure was Coal Hill School. Angular letters in orange crawled across the screen.

'The enemy is about to start moving,' came the gritty tones of the voice.

'You think Group Captain Gilmore suspects us?' asked Ratcliffe. 'Alerting the military now could cause problems.'

'Not the paltry military forces of your world – the real enemy: the imperial Dalek faction, Ven-Katri Davrett, may their shells be blighted. Soon it will be war.' The voice held a note of grim satisfaction. 'Are you ready for war, Mr Ratcliffe?' It was almost an accusation.

'Yes,' said Ratcliffe. 'This country fought for the wrong cause in the last war. When I spoke out they had me imprisoned.'

'You will be on the right side in this war.'

*

A soldier opened the door of the Mercedes and snapped a salute; Gilmore clambered out and returned it. He had managed a catnap during the short journey from Whitehall to Hendon – it was the only sleep he had been able to grab in the night and morning spent arguing with his superiors. In the end the Army, sensing a possible embarrassment for the Royal Air Force, had agreed.

He had been left for three hours in a musty Ministry of Defence anteroom as they deliberated. Dead generals in dark oil paintings stared down at him while he waited. The Air Marshal emerged from the conference room in a billow of cigar smoke. 'It's your show now,' he had said, passing Gilmore a thick sheaf of notes – the Rules of Engagement.

Gilmore was met by his batman at the entrance to Maybury Hall. 'Coffee,' he told the man, 'black, three sugars, in two minutes in my room.' The man nodded and scuttled off.

Gilmore strode up the corridor and opened the door to the duty room. Staff came to rapid attention in their seats. Sergeant Embery snapped to his feet. 'Evacuation plans,' Gilmore passed him the thick document, 'implementation immediate.'

The aroma of coffee filled his room. On the spare cot-bed, his batman had laid out fresh battle fatigues. The walnut handle of his service revolver protruded from the holster placed neatly on the folded squares of khaki cloth.

Gilmore washed in a white enamel basin with cold water from a matching jug. Cold brought a measure of sharpness back. Dressing brought him more into focus, making him more the man, more the soldier. But even the bitter coffee couldn't eliminate the subtle tang of fear in his mouth. He buckled on his gun belt with short savage tugs.

In a dimly lit hut twenty-three years ago, so newly built that it stank of resin, he had watched flickering green lines on a cathode ray tube as the WAAF operator intoned courses and speeds into her headset, a litany of Stukas. Within minutes the bombs had been falling among the box-girder radar towers. They had heard the screaming wail of a Stuka's dive, the death whistle of the bomb and the dull crump of the blast. The operator had calmly continued relaying flight information to Group Area Command, her soft voice never faltering until a bomb severed the landline.

That night he and the operator went down to the beach together. He had said her name over and over again as the terror abated into something else. The sea was a sheet of silver; small waves whispered over sand. 'Rachel,' he had said as the bombs went away.

Gilmore was transferred to training command in Scotland the next day. As he drove away he saw a formation of droning specks heading inland. Operator Jensen was already reporting their vectors to HQ in that soft calm voice of hers. Neither of them had ever married.

Gilmore pulled on his peaked cap. The badge was bright from polishing.

Rachel was studying the Doctor when the group captain came in. The little man was staring at the maps laid out on the billiard table – staring at, but not seeing them. It was as if he were studying another landscape that only he could see, planning moves on some unimaginable gaming board.

'Well, Doctor?' asked Gilmore.

'Group Captain,' said the Doctor. 'About the evacuation.'

'I have been in direct contact with High Command and they have agreed to a staged quiet withdrawal under the Peacetime Nuclear Accident Provisions. They felt that given the state of the current government…'

'Thanks to Miss Keeler,' said Allison.

'They felt, Miss Williams,' Gilmore looked sharply at the young woman, 'that the initial stages could be carried out under the aegis of the Intrusion Counter Measures Team. The D-notice committee has been informed and a cover story prepared.'

'What is it?' asked Rachel.

'I have no idea,' said Gilmore with surprise, 'not my department.'

Ask a stupid question, she thought.

'Now, Doctor,' Gilmore said briskly, 'since you hold my career in your hands, I hope you can justify my faith.'

'With respect, Group Captain,' said the Doctor, 'your career is magnificently irrelevant.'

Rachel saw Gilmore flinch as if he had been slapped. Emotions rippled across his face – anger and wounded pride. For a moment it was a face of a young lieutenant, lost on a moonlit beach. Then twenty-three years of memory clamped down and it became a warrior's mask again.

'Any more transmission sites?' the Doctor asked Rachel.

Rachel checked the map. 'Just the one at the school.'

'Good,' said the Doctor. 'I need a direct line to Jodrell Bank and, let me see,' his brow creased, '1963 – the Fylingdales installation.'

He seized a notepad and scribbled figures. 'Order them to search these localities for high orbital activity.' He gave Rachel the note: he had written six groups of three digits, meridian and polar co-ordinates.

'The detector vans should be moved so they can cover this area here and here.' He marked the maps with red crayon. 'All air and ground forces must be ordered to avoid engaging the enemy at all costs. We must act with extreme caution.'

'And if we don't?' asked Allison.

'Goodbye civilization as you know it.'

Ace was bored – really bored. The steam radio on the table was playing music that was all windy strings. Some jazz would be nice, a bit of go-go better, or even house or something by that trio of blonde bimbos whose name escaped her. Anything would be better than Dennis Boredom and his terminally tuneful string quartet. She had already tried the television, but all that showed was some woman with a posh accent thick enough to insulate cavity walls who played a piano while a wooden donkey jerked up and down.

And people get nostalgic about this decade, she thought. In seven years I'll be born; in twenty-four years I'll be sweating gelignite and something will happen

– what did the Doctor call it? – an 'adjustment'. An adjustment will happen and take me out of time. Ace decided she liked that. It could be worse: it could be Perivale.

Ace went to the window and pulled back the chintz curtain. A couple of boys were kicking a football around the street. She watched them, and then she noticed a square of cardboard in the window. It was hanging face outward; Ace took it off the hook and flipped it over. It was a hand-lettered sign which read:

NO COLOUREDS.

Ghost smell of disinfectant and charred wood.

Ace snatched up her jacket and rucksack, almost choking on the memories.

'I'm just going out for some *fresh* air,' she called out angrily. Not knowing or caring whether Mrs Smith heard, Ace ran out of the house, slamming the front door behind her.

'What's next on the list?' asked Mike.

Allison ran her finger down the sheet of paper attached to the clipboard. 'Parabolic reflector, twenty to thirty centimetres.'

'What's that in English?'

'Twelve inches or thereabouts.'

The Doctor had dashed off the list in the map room and handed it to Gilmore. He had handed it to Rachel, who, of course, had handed it to her. Allison and Mike had then scoured Maybury Hall for the varied array of items. Cannibalizing the messroom TV had not enhanced their popularity with the enlisted men.

'Where are we going to get a parabolic reflector?'

'Radio aerial,' suggested Mike.

'No, it says silvered, as in mirror. It's the last item.'

'I know, it's…' He stopped and waved his free hand around.

'On the tip of your tongue,' said Allison.

'Hot.'

'Cooker.'

'Warm.'

'What?'

'Like a cooker… electric…' he was getting quite frantic, 'ring… electric ring…'

'An electric heater?'

'Yes,' said Mike with relief.

'Why didn't you say so in the first place.'

Rachel watched the figures clatter onto the teleprinter: orbital co-ordinates, occlusion and estimated mass.

That can't be right, she thought.

The mass was given as four hundred thousand tonnes.

Oh my god! That was incredible!

A hand reached down and ripped the completed message off the machine.

'Here we are,' said the Doctor.

He sounds almost cheerful, thought Rachel. What does he know?

'It's a big mothership of some kind – could have as many as four hundred Daleks on board,' continued the Doctor. 'At least we know where it is.'

'Much good that does us,' said Rachel.

'It would be foolish of me, I suppose,' said Gilmore, 'to hope that this mothership is not nuclear capable.'

Doesn't he realize yet what we are dealing with, thought Rachel – engineering on that scale, technology beyond anything dreamed of.

'That ship has weapons capable of cracking this planet open like an egg.'

Allison and Mike banged through the doors with armfuls of junk. 'We got the parts you wanted, Doctor,' said Allison.

'Put them on the table.'

Rachel winced as delicate circuit boards tumbled onto the billiard table amid strips of metal, wires and unidentifiable components.

The Doctor pulled up a chair and sat facing the pile. Delicately he unrolled a wide suede strip on the table to reveal interesting looking tools that were held in place by loops and pouches. The Doctor picked up a circuit board and selected one of the tools.

'Is the mothership the Daleks' main base?' asked Gilmore.

'For one group at least,' said the Doctor, prising a transistor out of its socket. 'I suspect we are dealing with two possibly antagonistic Dalek factions.'

'Two?' queried Allison.

'But both come from outer space?' asked Gilmore.

'From another planet,' said the Doctor, 'and the distant future. We must try to contain both factions and let them destroy each other.'

Gilmore looked at the maps again and the big red

circle that defined the evacuation zone. 'Shouldn't we bring in reinforcements?' he asked. 'Armoured units…'

The Doctor cut him off. 'Haven't you listened to me, Group Captain? The ship up there has surveillance equipment that can spot a sparrow fall fifteen thousand kilometres away. Any sign of a military build up and they may decide to sterilize the area.'

Rachel suppressed a shudder at the word sterilize. It brought sudden pictures of Hiroshima to her mind: fabric patterns etched into flesh, people burnt away to nothing with only their shadows left to mark their existence.

'And we have no defence,' said Gilmore. It was a statement, not a question.

'Frightening, isn't it,' said the Doctor, 'to find that there are others better versed in death then human beings.'

The Doctor was making final adjustments to his contraption. It was an ungainly mixture of parts: there was the parabolic reflector of an electric fire at the front, from which wires led back into a maze of tubing.

'What does it do?' asked Rachel.

'At best it will interfere with a Dalek's internal controls,' said the Doctor. 'I rigged up something similar once on Spiridon.'

'And at worst?'

'It will do absolutely nothing.'

Spiridon, thought Rachel, fine.

Allison called over from the radio. 'Red Nine reports an increase in modulated signalling.'

The Doctor asked where. As Allison talked back to

Red Nine the Doctor beckoned Mike over. 'Call Ace and tell her that someone will pick her up.'

'The signal emanates from Coal Hill School,' called Allison. 'Multiple signals in close proximity.'

'Multiple?' said the Doctor. 'The transmat must be operational again.'

'Transmat?' asked Rachel. 'What does that mean?'

'Daleks,' said the Doctor.

Gilmore strode into the room, 'There's no reply from my men at the school.'

The Doctor stood up suddenly and started stuffing tools into his pockets. 'Get a vehicle ready and load it up with plastic explosives with integral detonators.'

Gilmore nodded and left.

'Why explosives?' asked Rachel.

The Doctor held up his contraption. 'This just disables them. What do you expect us to do then? Talk to them sternly?'

'Doctor,' said Mike, hanging up the phone, 'my mum says that Ace left ages ago.'

The Doctor was suddenly running for the door. Rachel and Mike looked at each other for a moment and ran after him. They caught up at the stairwell; the Doctor was taking the steps three at a time. He turned at the bottom and yelled up that Ace must be at the school.

'What makes you think she's got herself in danger?' gasped Rachel as she reached him.

The Doctor looked at her with such ferocious intensity that she recoiled. 'Of course she's got herself in danger,' he snapped, 'they always do.'

8
SATURDAY, 14:15

The dreamers awoke. Crab-shaped servo-robots scuttled over polycarbide armour, testing for defects. Power cables disengaged and retreated into the floor, clamps retracted and the warriors began gliding to the staging post.

Command data-net came on line; instructions in microsecond pulses flashed from relays. The last of the servo-robots dismounted, leaping from the warriors into their wall niches with cybernetic precision.

Doors opened.

The Daleks entered their designated transmat broadcast zones. Power shifted from the mothership's immense fusion reactor and energized the travelling field.

The first Dalek prepared to enter the combat zone.

Ace might have died.

Might have.

She had slipped into the quarantine zone, easily evading the squaddies who manned the checkpoints, and made her way to the school.

Outside a big Bedford truck sat untended; it was very quiet. Ace checked the cab: it was empty and the engine hood was cool and smelled of petrol. She assumed the soldiers were out patrolling or whatever it was that soldiers did when they were not saluting or shooting. She looked in the back just to be certain that they hadn't left any goodies behind, but was disappointed to find it empty. There wasn't even a whiff of explosives.

Ace found the tape deck where she had left it, on a bench in the chemistry lab. Just on the off-chance she flicked the selector to FM and switched on.

There was nothing but static at first. Then she heard a ghost of a metallic sound on the fringes of reception. Ace adjusted the frequency.

'Attack squad in position,' grated the unmistakable voice of a Dalek.

Ace froze. If the reception was that clear then the Daleks were close, possibly within the school itself.

Leaving the tape deck on, Ace ran for the stairs.

'Lower area clear,' the tape deck broadcast.

Ace collided with a wall and stopped, staring stupidly down the staircase. There was a movement on the landing below – a shadow.

A cream-coloured Dalek came round the corner.

Ace threw herself backwards just in time. An energy bolt carved a track through the space she had occupied and drilled a hole in the wall.

As she banged back into the lab, Ace heard the whine of the Dalek's motor unit as the creature prepared to ascend the stairs. She needed a plan and she needed it yesterday.

A distraction, she quickly thought.

Ace slammed a cassette into the tape deck, hit the play button, and twisted the volume to maximum.

A weapon.

Ace heard the Dalek's engine go into overdrive as it started up the stairs. She reached over her shoulder and felt the cool handle of the baseball bat. Ace slowly drew it out and backed behind the door.

The whine of the Dalek's engine was abruptly blotted out by two hundred watts of percussion.

Ace remained poised, bat upraised. A single trickle of sweat ran down her cheek; she could feel her heartbeat battering at her ribs. There was fear, but mixed in with that was anger, exhilaration and the absolute conviction of the young that they will live forever.

A Dalek forced its way through the doors. It was close enough for Ace to see her distorted reflection in the burnished gold of the creature's sensor pods. Even this close the Dalek made no noise as it zeroed in on the tape deck. Energy sprouted from its gunstick.

The tape deck exploded; a bench tap ruptured and water spewed out in a long arc.

The Dalek's eyestalk swivelled to scan the room.

'Small human female on level three.'

'Who are you calling small?' Ace brought the baseball bat down on the smooth dome. Neon blue tendrils of energy crackled as the bat hit, eating into the laminated surface. Slivers of armour exploded off the surface.

Ace struck the Dalek again before it could react – a glancing blow off the side.

The Dalek began to turn, describing a circle that would bring its weapon to bear.

Ace desperately swung the bat at the vulnerable eyestalk: there was a shower of sparks and the whole assembly parted from the dome and bounced away across the floor.

The Dalek screamed but kept turning. Ace threw herself under a bench; a stool bounced off her shoulder. Glass flasks exploded as the Dalek shot at Ace, tracking her by sound. A plume of flame shot upwards as a gas-tap was blown away.

Instinct told her to keep moving, but she was running out of classroom. She vaulted onto a bench, hoping to run past the Dalek and through the door. The Dalek fired again; the cabinet behind Ace exploded.

The Dalek blocked the doorway.

Ace pounded along the bench, the partition window rushing towards her. At the last moment she flung her arms in front of her face, screamed and jumped.

There was an agonizing moment of stillness.

Her forearms and then her shoulders silently bore the impact, and then she felt herself falling. The sharp crackle of breaking glass somewhere behind her shattered the silence, and then she bounced off the corridor wall.

The Dalek continued to scream and glass rained onto the floor as Ace scrambled to her feet. Bat still in hand she ran for the stairway, ignoring a sharp pain from her left ankle.

There was another Dalek at the top of the stairs.

Woman and Dalek saw each other at the same time.

Ace screamed as she charged forward.

The Dalek hesitated.

Ace gave it a vicious backhanded swing as she went past, and fragments of polycarbide exploded off the Dalek's casing. She took the staircase in two leaps, screaming again as she came down on her injured ankle.

She saw the dead soldier as she skidded into the entrance hall. Beside his sprawled body lay his gun and a rifle grenade. Ace grabbed the weapons and limped for the exit.

The commander of the Dalek attack squad had no name, yet it knew what it was. That was enough – it would always be enough. It puzzled over the reports from scouts one and two.

Scout one had sighted a small human female on level three. The commander had expected extermination details to follow, but scout one had instead registered severe damage. The female was using a weapon of advanced design and had disabled the scout. This was outside the parameters established for the operation.

Eight seconds after the attack on scout one, scout two sighted the female. It reported behaviour inconsistent with human response predictions.

The commander immediately tagged the female as an intruder human – one either not from this planet or from this temporal zone – or both. It recalled two undamaged warriors and assigned them intercept positions. Only one intruder was allowed for in the operational parameters – the Time Lord known as the Doctor. The commander issued a capture directive specified under the human section of Dalek battle tactics. The female was to be intimidated into surrender.

The commander entered the school entrance hall; it immediately sighted the female. The female now exhibited the expected reactions of fear and flight, accelerating away in the inefficient controlled fall of bipedal locomotion. The commander notified the two warriors to close in while it pursued the female.

As Ace entered the playground, the commander sprang its trap: it and the other warriors closed in on her. Again, the commander considered, the human deviated from normal human behavioural patterns, even as the intimidation took place.

'Exterminate!'

The voices rebounded off the walls and crowded Ace's mind; they made it difficult to think, harder to act.

'Exterminate!'

Three Daleks. There was a sickness in her stomach as she realized that blind aggression was not going to save her now. But why had they not killed her?

'Exterminate!'

The rifle was clumsy in her fingers; the grenade kept slipping off. She was determined to take one of them with her.

'Exterminate!'

They were on every side – an alien wall of white and gold. She knew she was going to die.

The Doctor is going to be really angry this time, she thought.

The commander monitored the female carefully, wary of more unpredictable behaviour. It contacted the mothership through the communications relay in the transmat below and demanded reinforcements.

It had just finished when communications were

drowned in static. Co-ordination systems suddenly malfunctioned; motor circuits failed to respond. With dimming vision the commander saw the female scuttle away. It tried to fire but its weapon failed. Wild power fluctuations disrupted the incubator, and it felt a sudden intense physical pain. There was a fleeting sensation of enemies, humans near itself.

Spiridon, it screamed silently, the Doctor.

Sudden heat and oblivion.

Ace fell down a few metres away from the Daleks. They were thrashing about, their gunsticks waving erratically. A weird moaning issued from somewhere deep within their shells.

Over the sound, Ace heard somone – was it Mike? – shouting orders. Then the Doctor cried: 'It worked!'

Figures in uniform darted among the Daleks, sticking grey plastic blobs on to the casings. Then they were gone.

'Get down,' shouted Mike.

Ace understood what the grey blobs were and threw her arms over her head.

There was a deafening noise and it started raining bits of Dalek.

9

Perhaps the most notable of the Cambridge Group in the 1950s was Professor Rachel Jensen. Hardly recognized outside the scientific community despite her pivotal work with Turing during the war, she retired suddenly in 1964. Her autobiography *The Electrical Dreamer* is curiously vague as to why. She married a year later.

The Women That Science Forgot
by Rowan Sesay (1983)

Three explosions occurred in quick succession: smoke belched out of the entrance to the covered playground. Three white and gold Daleks had brewed up in the confined space. Rachel clutched a carbon dioxide extinguisher and dashed into the smoke. There was an unidentifiable stench that reminded her of burning fat.

The Doctor stared at the shattered Daleks, his face unreadable.

'There were living beings in there,' he said.

Mike looked at the smoking remains. 'Not any more.'

Gilmore holstered his gun and turned to Mike. 'Search the area upstairs.'

Mike took from the Doctor the device that had

confused the Daleks and led a squad into the school buildings.

Rachel beckoned to Allison and they cautiously approached the trio of Daleks. The top dome of one had been blown off by the plastic explosive. Smears of carbon ran down the shoulder flanges, and vapour rose from the shattered bowl at the top. Rachel thought she saw something move amid the tangle of wiring.

'Doctor,' called Rachel, backing away and pulling Allison with her. 'I think this one is still active.'

The Doctor hurried over. Something clattered under Allison's foot – Ace's baseball bat. The Doctor peered into the steaming interior of the Dalek.

Rachel heard something – a sharp scuttling movement in the interior.

'Interesting,' breathed the Doctor.

Rachel backed further away from the Dalek, picking her way through the metal and organic scraps scattered over the rough concrete.

The sound inside the Dalek ceased, and the Doctor leaned closer for a better look. Rachel suppressed the urge to scream.

A grey-green thing reared out of the Dalek and lashed out at the Doctor – it was a twisted claw. Rachel screamed. Grey ropy strands erupted around the claw as it fastened on the Doctor's throat.

Allison fell backwards, fumbling for something on the ground. Tubes – or were they veins? – pulsed on the spindly wrist, the bony fingers clutching at the Doctor's neck. His hands were pulling at the gripping claw, his face was beginning to mottle.

Then Allison was beside him, her arm swinging down, the baseball bat an arc of silver. Energy exploded from the shrivelled arm. The Dalek screamed. Allison hit it again and again. She kept on bringing down the bat, and each time liquid spattered her face and the walls.

'Allison,' said the Doctor.

Allison upended the bat and savagely ground it into the Dalek. There was a grisly crunching sound.

'Allison,' said the Doctor, restraining her. 'It's dead.'

Allison flinched. There was a clatter as the bat fell to the ground.

'Thank you,' the Doctor said softly, leading her away from the Dalek.

'What was that?' said Rachel. It seemed an inadequate thing to say.

'They've mutated again.' The Doctor calmly inspected the stinking cavity. 'Here, have a look.' He made space for her. 'It's all right, it's dead now. Compare this with the destroyed Dalek at Totter's Lane. Look at the differences.'

Ace checked herself for injuries. Her leg was painful and on her upper arm there was a nasty bruise which she had got when she smashed through the window. Her ribs hurt – she took a deep breath but there was no sharp pain. No ribs broken then, she thought. Carefully, Ace picked a sliver of glass from her jacket sleeve and considered getting up.

Just give it a few seconds, she decided, to get my breath back. She wasn't yet ready to face the Doctor. She watched as Rachel stooped over the Dalek.

'The other Dalek was underdeveloped,' said Rachel, 'with vestigial limbs and sensory organs, almost amoeboid. This is altogether different, it has functional appendages with some kind of mechanical prosthesis grafted on to its body.'

Functional appendages, thought Ace, remembering the claw, that's one way of putting it.

Rachel's face had collapsed in disgust. 'I think I'm going to be sick.'

Ace decided to draw attention to herself. She tried to get up. 'Don't anyone give me a hand.'

Allison rushed over. 'You're hurt?'

'I had an argument with a window.'

The Doctor was suddenly there kneeling beside her. He motioned Allison away. 'You two had better check the cellar, but don't touch anything.'

He stared at them, watching until they went. Then he turned to Ace.

Now I'm going to get it, she thought.

'When I say stay put, I mean stay put,' said the Doctor, 'not take on an entire Dalek assault squad single-handed.' He ran practised fingers along Ace's leg, checking the damage. Before Ace could stop him he hooked one palm under her knee and brought it sharply upwards. The leg twinged.

Ace gasped.

'Why did you come here?' asked the Doctor.

'I left my tape deck here.'

'Where is it now?'

Good question! she thought. 'In little bits,' she said ruefully.

'Good,' said the Doctor.

'What do you mean "good"?' Ace was astonished. 'Where am I going to get another one?'

'Your tape deck was a dangerous anachronism. If somebody had found it and discovered the principles of its function the whole microchip revolution would take place twenty years too early, with uncalculable damage to the timeline.'

'So?' said Ace sullenly.

'Ace,' said the Doctor, 'the Daleks have a starship up there with the capability of erasing this planet from space. But even they, ruthless though they are, would think twice before making such a radical alteration to the timeline.'

There's more to this time travel lark then meets the eye, decided Ace.

The Doctor reached out and pinched the lobe of her ear, once.

'You should be able to get around on that leg now.'

Ace carefully got to her feet and tested her weight on the leg. It was still a bit shaky but the pain had gone.

'Cheers, Professor.'

The Doctor smiled and picked up the baseball bat.

Rachel and Allison stood in the cellar and stared at the alien machine. Rachel's fingers were itching. Inside the machine were secrets that could reshape the world. She wanted to get in there and have a good look at its guts.

'The subject obviously is placed on the dais,' said Allison. 'Then what?'

'The Doctor called it a transmat,' said Rachel. 'What

does that imply to you?'

'Matter transmission, but that's…'

'Impossible,' said Rachel glumly. 'You know, after this is over I'm going to retire and grow begonias.'

'Lovely flowers, begonias,' said the Doctor from the stairs.

'Doctor,' said Allison, 'how exactly does this thing work?'

'Don't bother,' said Rachel.

The Doctor stepped over to the transmat and casually ran his hand over it. 'It's a link for the Daleks, allowing them to beam attack squads on to Earth without anyone knowing it.'

He shook his head and raised the baseball bat as if feeling the weight of it. He smiled and then smashed the baseball bat down on the control panel: metal crumpled, energy flared off the bat, and coloured panels shattered. There was a stink of ozone. 'And I don't want them here just yet.' He punctuated every word with the baseball bat. There was a splintering sound and the end of the bat flew off. It ricocheted off a wall and fell at Rachel's feet. 'Hah – weapons,' the Doctor looked at the remains of the handle, 'always useless in the end.'

He looked at Rachel. She stared at him. Those remarkable eyes of his were full of energy.

'Come on,' he said, 'there are things to be done.'

Mike came down the stairs smiling. When he saw Ace, the smile became wider.

'I found this upstairs,' he said, producing a Dalek eyepiece from behind his back, 'in the chemistry lab.

One of the Daleks seems to have lost it.'

Ace took the eyepiece from him, tossed it end over end and caught it. 'I wonder how that happened?'

'Somebody must have knocked it off,' said Mike, 'with a blunt instrument.'

Ace tossed the eyepiece up again. A hand snapped out and caught it in mid-air.

'Where's Gilmore?' said the Doctor.

'He's coming,' said Mike, gesturing at the stairs.

The Doctor waved the eyepiece at Ace. 'It's dangerous to play with Daleks, even bits of Daleks,' he said and threw the eyepiece over his shoulder.

Gilmore emerged from the stairwell. 'The area is clear of Daleks. How should we proceed from here?'

'I think,' said the Doctor, 'before we proceed anywhere, I should consult my assistant.'

He pulled Ace out of earshot. 'We're facing a very serious crisis. Destroying the transmat won't hold the white Daleks very long.'

'I could brew up some nitro-nine,' said Ace.

'I think it's gone a little beyond that now,' said the Doctor.

Mike leaned over and said to Allison: 'What's he up to now.'

'Something Machiavellian,' said Allison.

'Something what-ian?'

Rachel looked at the Doctor's back. He was making small sharp gestures; Ace was nodding. 'I think he's playing games, very dangerous games.'

Gilmore nodded. 'He seems to know what he is

doing.' It was said grudgingly.

Rachel looked back at the Doctor. 'But Group Captain,' she said, 'do we know what he's doing?'

10
SATURDAY, 15:00

The technological renaissance on Skaro briefly made the ageing planet once again the centre of Dalek cultural life, in so far as it can be said that a race like the Daleks can have a culture. This was its short flowering before the inevitable fall.

> *The Children of Davros, a Short History*
> *of the Dalek Race, Vol XX*
> by Njeri Ngugi (4065)

It was called the *Eret-mensaiki Ska*, Destiny of Stars. The flagship of the Imperial Fleet, it was constructed in orbit round Skaro. Elegant in conception and execution, it typified the Dalek renaissance.

Now it ran quietly, locked into geostationary orbit by the ceaseless murmering of its thrusters. Passive sensors soaked up data from the planet below like a sponge.

The systems co-ordinator was alone at the centre of the bridge, the Dalek's adapted manipulator arm plugged into the console before it. Through the interface it monitored the many functions on the vast ship. In a fundamental way, it was the ship.

With a small part of its mind it adjusted the nutrient

drip in the birthing creche, balancing the protein levels in the feed tubes that led to the gestation capsules. Inside each duralloy bubble a perfect Dalek foetus contentedly gurgled to the soft whine of the indoctrination tapes.

The systems co-ordinator monitored a servo-robot as it scuttled across the vast port flank of the ship, quickly sealing meteorite punctures with tiny squirts of gel.

A hull-mounted missile launcher twitched in its socket testing its orientation.

Radiation sensors inside the burning heart of the fusion generator spiked twice and then subsided.

All this barely broke the surface of the co-ordinator's consciousness, as subliminal to it as breathing was once to its humanoid ancestors.

The focus of its attention lay two hundred kilometres below, priority red, watching for the sign.

Waiting.

'I don't think Group Captain Gilmore is very happy,' said Ace.

'He's a military man,' said the Doctor. 'Lack of action makes his brain seize up.'

Ace looked over at the other table where Gilmore was sitting with Rachel and Allison. Harry's best effort lay uneaten in front of him. She caught Rachel staring at the Doctor again; the scientist quickly looked away when she noticed Ace.

Mike laughed, the sound muffled by the sausage he was eating. His fork stabbed at the air, punctuation for his humour. He saw Ace watching and covered his mouth with his hand. Ace looked down at her mixed grill. What she needed was some toast.

The Doctor was staring ahead, his brow creased. Ace had seen this look before.

The Doctor was waiting for something to happen.

George Ratcliffe was good at waiting.

He learned to be patient in prison while the rest of England waged senseless war against the one nation that should have been its ally. He had been reviled by the very people he'd been fighting to save.

They had called him a traitor.

Men that had stood shoulder to shoulder with him in the 1930s – good men who had marched down Cable Street, proud to be English, proud to fight against the Jew and the Bolshevik, proud to stand up for their race – even they had rejected him, blinded by the Zionist propaganda. Ratcliffe found himself alone, a single voice against the madness.

And so he had gone to prison under Regulation 18b and learned patience; he had been rewarded.

A few spots of drizzle fell on his face. Around him gravestones marked generations of dead Englishmen. In the distance, birds sang. Ratcliffe walked slowly down the main path. The sky threatened rain.

Third on the left, thought Ratcliffe, and stopped.

The grave was unremarkable. The headstone bore a single mark – the Greek symbol for Omega.

The Hand of Omega, thought Ratcliffe, destiny and power.

Ratcliffe's business as a building merchant prospered in the 1950s. The East End had been mauled during the

Blitz. There was a lot of work and Ratcliffe still had his contacts.

Rebuilding the Association proved harder. The influx of new immigrants helped. They were easy targets, more obvious than the Jews, more different. Yet it was not like the 1930s – there was affiuence now. People didn't need scapegoats like they used to. Ratcliffe knew in his heart that the Association would never amount to more than a rabble driven by hatred.

But that was before *they* arrived. Then everything had changed.

Rachel sipped her coffee: it was cold.

'I just feel we should be doing something,' said Gilmore.

'I wouldn't advise it,' said Rachel. 'We're in way over our heads already.'

'You were designated chief scientific adviser – one tends to expect some advice from one's advisers.'

Oh really, she thought.

'For one thing, Group Captain, I was not hired, I was drafted. And for another, do you think I'm enjoying having some space vagrant come along and tell me that the painstaking research I've devoted my life to has been superseded by a bunch of tin-plated pepperpots?'

'Steady on, Professor.'

'Steady on?' Rachel had trouble keeping her voice down. 'You drag me down from Cambridge, quote the Peacetime Emergency Powers Act at me and then expect me to advise on a situation that is outside the realm of human experience. Bluntly, Group Captain, we are reliant on the Doctor, because only the Doctor knows what is going on.'

Gilmore glanced at the Doctor, who was still sitting with his chin on his hands and looking into space. 'Well, I wish he would tell us.'

So do I, thought Rachel, so do I. She took another sip of coffee: it was still cold.

Ratcliffe needed something to probe the grave. He wasn't going to drag his men down here and dig up a grave in broad daylight. Not until he was sure that what he wanted was down there.

He found a loose rail, part of the brass ornamental surround of a nearby grave. It was rusty and came away easily. He raised it above his head and, with a last look at the Omega symbol on the headstone, plunged it into the earth.

The Omega device felt the disturbance in the earth above it and responded with sudden eagerness. It snapped out a tendril of itself and probed. A thin lattice of heavy iron atoms, streaked with oxide impurities. This analysis was unnecessary, its parameters for response included any deliberate disturbance. There was a subtle shift in one part of the device's matrix as it considered the implications and formulated the proper response.

This took a nanosecond.

It reconfigured part of its substance, drew power from its reserves.

And howled.

*

Ace watched as the Doctor smiled grimly.

An externally mounted sensor on the *Eret-mensaiki Ska* overloaded and went dead. Emergency systems shut down other equally sensitive sensors, but not before three more flared and died. There was a flurry of activity as medium range detectors cast around for the source, locking on with Dalek efficiency.

A point flared like a small sun on the three-dimensional grid-map of the world below. It was a power source, radiating energy at such levels that the ship's automatic defences responded as if the vessel were under attack.

The systems co-ordinator was bombarded with a rush of data. It quivered in its shell as atrophied glands released adrenalin into its body.

Power source detected. Its amplified thoughts coursed through the com-net – *full alert.* The signal radiated out of the bridge in a controlled chain-reaction.

The alert bridge crew slammed into their connections. Neuro-receptors engaged into command jacks. The system operator shunted scanner, weapon and defence functions over to the bridge crew.

Scan-op quickly tested the signal and reported: *It is the Omega device.*

The systems co-ordinator made its decision.

Inform the Emperor.

The girl skipped through the cemetery. The gravestones shifted like ghosts to her augmented eyes, their shapes overlaid with different, alien meanings. She was so charged with energy that she couldn't feel her feet touch the ground.

She rounded the church and vaulted the iron railing that surrounded it. Her legs easily absorbed the impact of the landing, transforming the energy into a forward vector with machine-like precision. Her eyes scanned the lines of stones: she had a function to perform.

The girl saw activity and ran towards it.

It happened.

For a second she had no legs; she squirmed in liquid confinement. Thoughts burrowed their way into her mind, her reflexes slowed by pain.

She was lying on the ground, breathing in the grass.

It had happened before.

The girl got up, her nausea overridden by control. She picked up the target activity and became flush with power again.

A group of humans worked at a grave. One of them had a name and designation – Ratcliffe, quisling. He was shouting at the other humans digging in the grave, urging them to work faster. Then he saw the girl.

'What are you staring at?'

He remembered being a man. The blue-white sun that burned over the mountains on the long summer evenings. A childhood, adolescence among the debris of Kaled encampments, games of Hunt the Thal played with sticks and mutant beetles. His indoctrination and training, a glittering career, the Elite cadre, lovers, adrenalin, blood, bone, sinew, feelings.

Ended by the war.

Ended by a Thal shell and a rush of radioactivity.

He remembered the smell of his own blood, pulsing slowly from severed arteries, the taste of concrete dust in his mouth, and the crackling of his own skin. He hurtled blindly into darkness.

And then resurrection.

An age of pain and humiliation. He was reconstructed with chrome and plastic, held together by tungsten wire. They drilled sockets through his skull and threaded fibre-optics into his forebrain.

He screamed when he saw himself for the first time. The med-techs smashed him back into darkness with anaesthetic. Questions were raised among the Kaled Elite: for all his brilliance, should such an abomination be allowed to live? The psych-techs said there was an eighty-six per cent probability, plus or minus ten per cent, that he would commit suicide within an hour of waking. A decision was made – let the creature prove his function, or die.

They allowed him awareness once more and he looked at himself again. The Elite gave him a trigger linked to a lethal dose of poison and then they left him.

He spent a long time examining the monstrosity he had become, searching for some reason to live. His remaining hand trembled on the switch that would kill him. With a convulsive effort he twisted himself into his new shape. I am but the idea, he thought, the seed, the dream. He saw a purity, not in what he was, but in what he might become. A being unbound by flesh and the stupidities that flesh brings. A creature fit to hold dominion.

Carefully he put the trigger down. At a thought his chair turned, a door opened and he slid out to face the Elite. 'Give me what I want,' he told them, 'and I will give you victory.' They provided for him, of course. It was their destiny to serve his purpose.

Emperor on the bridge.

Now the low vibration of the Dalek ship sang a song of power as he entered.

Report, he ordered.

Scan-op shunted data. *We have located the Omega device.*

Tac-op went on line, estimated troop deployments, native and renegade, updated battle senarios, bombardment patterns. *Renegade agents are in the area*, it reported.

Prepare the assault shuttle, ordered the Emperor. *They will surrender the Omega device or be exterminated.*

The girl was beginning to irritate Ratcliffe. Her cool gaze was making him uncomfortable. 'Haven't you got a home to go to?' he demanded.

She just stared back – unblinking, Ratcliffe realized with a prickling of the flesh on his neck. He turned back to his men. 'Put your backs into it,' he shouted. 'We don't have all day.'

He could feel the girl's eyes on his back. He turned, ready to lash out, threaten – anything to make her leave.

The girl was gone.

With a sudden thrill Ace saw the Doctor come to life. With a small movement of his hand he summoned

Gilmore over. The cafe became suddenly quiet and expectant.

Now that's style, thought Ace.

'We need to establish a forward base at the school,' said the Doctor. 'Can it be done?'

Gilmore nodded quickly and turned to Mike. 'Sergeant, get Embery. Move in command units.' Ace could hear the confidence creeping back into Gilmore's voice. 'Establish forward command, third floor, defensive positions on the ground floor and the roof.'

Mike hesitated over his second plate of chips.

'Get a move on,' snapped Gilmore, and Mike moved.

The Doctor's eyes were intense as the soldiers began boiling out of the cafe. He's doing it again, thought Ace.

Rachel felt suddenly cold when she saw Ace grin.

'Professor Jensen, Miss Williams,' said Gilmore.

'Ja wohl,' said Allison quietly and stood up. 'Coming, Professor Jensen?'

Rachel put down her coffee and grabbed her coat. 'Of course Miss Williams.' I wouldn't miss this for the world, she thought.

'I wish Bernard was here.'

'The British Rocket Group has its own problems.'

Ace sidled over to the counter and pinched a piece of toast.

'What's so important about the school?'

'Now that I've disabled the imperial Daleks' transmat,' said the Doctor, 'absolutely nothing. The renegade Daleks have the Hand of Omega and all Dalek attention will be focused on that.'

'Oh.'

The Doctor gave her a suspicious look. 'Well?'

'Nothing.'

The Doctor stood up.

'There is one thing.'

'What?'

'What are we doing?'

'Ah,' said the Doctor and turned to leave.

I should have expected that, thought Ace. She decided it was time to look for more explosives.

Ratcliffe's yard was situated down Pullman's Road, a narrow little backstreet. As the truck negotiated the tricky corner into the yard, Ratcliffe found himself whistling Wagner.

In the back, with the rest of his men, was the Hand of Omega. Now he knew he had something to bargain with. Now he could ask for the world.

For months 'it' had nestled in the corner of his office. He had just walked in one day and found it there masked by shadow – a vague mechanical shape, a voice that gave him secrets. It gave him secrets and the promise of power.

He stepped down from the truck.

'Charlie?'

'Yeah.'

'Get the damn thing off the truck and put it over on the trestles.'

'But it's cold,' said Charlie.

'So wear your gloves.' Charlie was loyal, but a few

coupons short of a pop-up toaster.

Ratcliffe slammed the sliding door over and went into the warehouse. There was a musty smell from the racks of timber – he hadn't done much work recently. He hadn't needed to, what with the money 'it' had supplied. He opened the door to his office and entered.

'We have the Hand of Omega,' he said. 'It's out in the yard.'

'Excellent.'

Ratcliffe sat down at his desk and picked up the telephone receiver. 'I'll tell my man. After all, he found it for us.' He sat back in the chair and watched as the phone dialled itself.

The sun had broken through the clouds, splashing light across the playground. Four soldiers were piling up sandbags by the front door. Ace glimpsed khaki boxes stacked against the wall. One big box was open, revealing a long tube nestling in straw. A recoilless anti-tank gun, she thought, classy.

'If this place is so out of the way of the action,' she asked the Doctor, 'what are we all doing here?'

'I want to keep an eye on the group captain,' said the Doctor. He pushed open the doors.

The entrance hall was full of noise. Field telephone cables snaked across the floor, disappearing through doorways. A soldier was nailing up signs indicating the operations room, the mess, and one crudely lettered 'KHAZI'. Down the hall someone was swearing in a foreign language. Ace peered past a group of soldiers hefting ammunition boxes to see Rachel. She was gesticulating at two soldiers who were trying to lift a huge box of electronics up the back stairs. Allison was watching her colleague with an astonished expression. There was a smell of packing straw, sweat and overboiled tea.

Rachel ran out of Yiddish profanities and resorted to glaring at the privates' backs. Allison was wincing every time the computer banged against the floor.

'This is stupid,' said Rachel, 'where's Sergeant Smith?'

'I can see Ace,' said Allison.

'We want to move the thing,' said Rachel, 'not blow it up.'

'There he is.'

Mike emerged from a classroom. He saw Ace and stopped. His eyes followed her as she disappeared up the stairwell.

'He fancies her, doesn't he?' said Allison.

'It's her Aryan looks.'

There was a loud crash from behind them and the sound of delicate electronics breaking. Rachel didn't bother to turn round.

'Allison?'

'Yes?'

'How's your mental arithmetic?'

'This reminds me of parties I used to go to,' said Ace. She was sitting on the stairs with the Doctor. From below they could hear the sound of frantic military activity. 'They're really busting a gut down there.'

'That's the general idea,' said the Doctor. 'I want to

keep the military fully occupied and out of the way.'

'Out of the way of what?' Ace kicked at a bit of loose paint on the wall. 'Professor, you promised, remember?'

'A long time ago, on my home planet of Gallifrey, there was a stellar engineer called Omega…'

The prelaunch checks were complete. Omega settled his big frame into the shock webbing. The sound of the big engines could be heard despite the capsule's layers of shielding. 'What's Rassilon doing?' Omega asked the other with him.

'Going over the data,' said the other.

'Again?'

'He worries.'

Omega was silent for a moment. 'How about you?'

'Stellar!' said Ace. 'As in stars – you mean he engineered stars?'

'Ace.'

'Sorry, go on.'

'It was Omega who created the supernova that formed the initial power source for Gallifreyan time travel experiments. He left behind him the basis on which Rassilon founded Time Lord society, and the Hand of Omega.'

'His hand? What good is that?'

'Not his hand literally, no, it's called that because Time Lords have an infinite capacity for pretension.'

The engines were whining, the vortex could almost be felt eating away at the fabric of space and time. 'Stop fussing and get out,' Omega told the other.

'I have doubts.'

'You always have doubts.' Omega's grin was fierce. 'You're as bad as Rassilon.' He flexed his great hands and placed them on the control interface. 'Doubts will chain you in the end.' The engines were screaming now. 'We'll see who's remembered in the histories.'

'I've noticed that,' said Ace.

'The Hand of Omega is the mythical name for Omega's remote stellar manipulator – the device he used to customize stars.'

Ace suddenly understood. 'The Daleks want it so they can recreate the time travel experiments.' She was missing something. 'Hold on, you said both Dalek factions can already travel in time.'

'They have time corridor technology,' said the Doctor. 'But it's very crude and nasty. What the Daleks want is the power over time that the Time Lords have. That's what the Hand of Omega will give them,' he smiled, 'or so they think.'

'And you have to stop them.'

'I want them to have it.'

'Eh?'

'My main problem is stopping Group Captain Gilmore and his men getting killed in the cross-fire.'

'So all this is…'

'A massive deception,' said the Doctor. 'Yes.'

'That's well devious.' And it was, except why does he want the Daleks to have the Hand of Omega? If she asked him direct she would get an evasion. 'So the

Daleks grab the Hand of Omega and nobody gets hurt. Well brilliant.'

Omega was screaming. The control room was silent – everyone knew he was dead; this was just the distant echo of his dying. A new star flared in the sky. One of the controllers made the ward sign against evil.

'Stop that,' screamed Rassilon at the controller. 'No superstition.' His face was contorted with emotion, and for a moment it looked as if he would strike the controller. 'Do not profane his memory now – not now.' Rassilon's voice broke and he stumbled away.

The other looked at the new star on the main screen. The expanding shell of matter was picked out in red by computer enhancement – an accidental rendering of the regenerative circle, the ancient symbol of death.

'You've got your place in the histories now,' he said softly, and turned away.

'There's just one problem,' said the Doctor.

'What?'

'I wasn't expecting two Dalek factions.' He stood up. 'Now we have to make sure that the wrong Daleks don't run away with it.'

This could be fun, she thought. 'Shouldn't we take Mike?'

'No. Dalek hunting is a terminal pastime.'

'So what are we doing then?'

'Dalek hunting.'

Ask a stupid question, Ace thought.

*

The assault team marshalled in the shuttle bay. They were the cream of the *Ven-Katri Davrett* warriors – imperial Dalek stormtroopers.

The commander watched them as they loaded section by section, gleaming perfection after gleaming perfection. It felt something akin to pride.

When they loaded the Abomination, the commander felt such distate that its gunstick involuntarily twitched. So strongly did it feel that it almost queried the loading order. But only almost – a Dalek did not query Tac-op orders more than once and remain functional.

We shall win this battle without the Abomination, decided the commander, we shall prove our function.

The shuttle prepared to launch.

The supreme renegade Dalek had lived in the darkness of Ratcliffe's warehouse for many months. Its secondary systems had been shut down all that time as it lived by proxy through its link with the battle computer.

Sometimes it dreamed. They were frightening unnatural dreams – dreams in which it walked like a biped, naked to the environment, breathing unfiltered air.

Psychological programs within the Dalek's computer countered the dreams with increasing amounts of sedatives that left it agitated within its protective shell. Technical analysis made the source clear – battle computer feedback. This had not been foreseen at the planning stage – a great deal had not been foreseen. The arrival of the imperial warship, the destruction of the warrior at Totters Lane, the involvement of native military forces.

They were pernicious these bipeds, these *humans* with their talent for violence and sudden improvisation. They made dangerous slaves.

The battle computer reported that the Hand of Omega was in place. The Dalek Supreme snapped out of dormancy, power flushed through its systems – it felt alive again. The battle computer flashed a tactical update, and based on this the Dalek Supreme made decisions and issued orders. Around it, other warriors became operational. Sensitive aural sensors detected noise from the yard outside – the unlovely sound of human laughter. These were the native bipeds that had carried the Hand of Omega. They were now disposable.

The Dalek Supreme fed power to its motor unit and slipped forward.

'What people need,' said Ratcliffe, 'is a firm hand. It's in their nature. They need a strong leader, someone who knows when to be lenient and when to be harsh…'

He was cut off by the sound of men screaming.

Outside, he thought, and lunged across the office and threw open the door.

His men were lying smashed and broken on the cobbles.

'What have you done?' he screamed. 'They were my men.' There was movement from the shadow in the corner. 'They were on our side.'

The shadow rotated, and for the first time Ratcliffe could make out its shape. Something unfolded from the darkness and emerged into the glow from his desk lamp. Light glinted on pale hair, pale skin and blue eyes.

'You are a slave,' said the girl. 'You were born to serve the Daleks.'

11

The Movellan War was the most disastrous military campaign the Daleks fought. It is perhaps fitting that it took an android race to perceive the Daleks' ultimate weakness. When the blow came it took the Daleks' strategic planners by surprise. They had used biological weapons against many races, in the Spiridon campaign, for example. It never occurred to the Daleks that they might be vulnerable to bacteriological warfare.

The Daleks suffered eighty-three per cent casualties. The great empire that had dominated so much of Mutter's Spiral disintegrated overnight. Its great battlefleets were shattered, its industrial base gone like smoke, and the Daleks' homeworld [Skaro] isolated. Remnants of the sector commands became the various factions that characterize Dalek politics to this day…

… the Daleks attempted to use their time corridor technology to repair the damage but to no avail… it was Davros's subversion of the imperial Skarosian Daleks that opened the schism between them and the renegades. The unthinkable became reality – civil war.'

The Children of Davros, Vol XIX
by Njeri Ngugi (4065)

Ace flattened herself against the side of the car, cold metal under her palms. She could feel the Doctor as a tense presence beside her. Ace risked a look over the bonnet. A grey Dalek went silently past, followed by two more, moving quickly down the road.

That makes six so far, thought Ace. Where are they coming from?

The Doctor tapped her shoulder. 'This way,' he said, and moved off.

Ace followed the Doctor away from the parked car. Gardens backed onto the street on one side, the other side was lined with warehouses. The Doctor led her towards a set of open gates marked in white letters:

Ratcliffe and Co Ltd
Roofing and construction

'The main staging area must be in that warehouse,' said the Doctor.

'Are we going to have a look?' asked Ace.

'Might as well,' said the Doctor.

Ace caught a glimpse of something moving behind one of the gates. 'Look out.'

There were no cars to hide behind here. The Doctor snagged her with his umbrella and pulled her back against the wall. There was a wooden door; the Doctor gave a sharp shove at the lock and the door sprang open. A small china sign warned them to beware of the dog.

'In here,' said the Doctor, hustling Ace through. She quickly closed the door behind them and turned around. They were in a long, narrow, well-kept garden. Washing was hung out on a white line, there was no sign of movement from the house. A large Alsation sat on the lawn and watched them.

'Nice doggie,' Ace said hopefully.

The Doctor watched the street through a knot-hole.

'I think that's the lot,' said the Doctor after a minute. He opened the door and stepped into the street. The Alsation watched them go with incurious eyes.

'So where are they?' Gilmore could feel things slipping out of his control.

'I've checked the whole building, sir,' said Mike. 'They've gone.'

Gilmore didn't need this, not now, not with the Ministry of Defence breathing down his neck. A square mile of Shoreditch had been evacuated. They wouldn't be able to keep a lid on events forever, whatever the cover story. And now the Doctor had taken it in his head to vanish, just when Gilmore needed him.

He told Mike to deploy look-outs. 'And then take a squad and sweep the area,' he added. He caught Rachel's eye; she looked worried. 'I want the Doctor found and brought back here.'

There was a tangle of bodies in the yard – four or five men in work clothes were sprawled on the cobbles, their limbs twisted in unnatural positions. The Doctor knelt quickly and lifted a man's wrist.

'Daleks,' he said, and for a moment Ace saw a terrible anger in his face. The Doctor let go and the arm fell limply back. Ace heard a faint humming sound. Behind the bodies was a casket set on crude wooden trestles – the sound was coming from there. As the Doctor approached the hum grew in intensity. 'Be quiet,' he said to the casket; the sound diminished.

'Is that it?' asked Ace.

The Doctor placed a hand on the pitted metal and smiled. 'The Hand of Omega – the most powerful and sophisticated remote stellar manipulation device ever constructed – is in here.'

Ace glanced at the bodies. 'Are you sure you want the Daleks to have it?'

'Absolutely,' said the Doctor.

Ace picked her way through the bodies and touched the casket with her hand. There was a tingling sensation in her fingertips and it was cold.

'You know what to do, don't you?' The Doctor was talking to the casket. 'Yes, of course you do.'

He talks to it as if it were…

'It's alive?'

The Doctor nodded. 'In a manner of speaking.' He walked to a big pair of sliding doors. 'You don 't mess about with the interior of stars unless you have some intelligence.' There was a normal sized door set into the larger sliding ones. 'It's less intelligent than the prototype, though. That one was so smart it went on strike for better conditions.'

The Doctor opened the door and beckoned Ace in.

Inside it was dim. She could make out a big storeroom

whose shelves were piled with wooden planks, trays of nails and paint pots. Ace saw that it was all covered in a thin layer of dust; it smelt of resin and paint-stripper. Down a short connecting corridor she could see what looked like an office.

The Doctor checked to see if anyone was about and stepped in. The office contained a desk, a chair, a filing cabinet and something else. Ace immediately recognized it as Dalek technology.

Somebody sits in it, she thought, and the helmet fits over their head. She started to climb onto the seat. Whoever uses this thing is small – like a kid.

The Doctor pulled her away. 'What is it?' she asked.

The Doctor looked at the chair thing. 'Some kind of biomechanoid control centre,' he said, 'Adapted for a small human.' He examined one of the connecting fibres. 'Of course – it's a battle computer.'

'Why would a human need to sit in it?'

'The Daleks' major drawback is their dependence on logic and rationality.' The Doctor grinned. 'All you have to do is make a couple of irrational moves and the Daleks get confused.'

'You mean they're too clever by half?'

The Doctor ignored her. 'Their solution is to get a humanoid, preferably young and imaginative, plug him into the system and his intuition and creativity are slaved to the battle computer.'

'It's well boggling.'

'It's obscene,' said the Doctor. 'Now for their time controller.' He reached behind the desk and pulled open a drawer.

'What is it?'

It was a globe with lightning at its centre. 'It's the device they use to travel through time.' He looked into its heart. 'They've come a long way.' The Doctor placed his hands on the globe. Lightning clung to his fingertips. Ace saw his shoulders tense as he seemed to push with his arms.

The globe went dark.

'Have you broken it?'

The Doctor looked at her with surprise. 'No,' he said, 'I don't want to lumber Earth with a Dalek battle squad. I merely put it out of phase. They can fix it but it will slow them down.'

The Doctor flexed his fingers. A white rectangle appeared like a playing card in the hand of a conjurer. It, however, was smaller than a playing card – more like a gentleman's calling card. The Doctor placed it by the time controller. There was strange angular writing on the card.

Ace heard a noise. It was time to leave.

Something was wrong.

Outside of the battle computer, data transmission was imperfect. The interface between the girl and the Dalek Supreme blurred further.

Something was wrong.

The Dalek Supreme re-entered the operations centre. The girl moved with biped agility to the time controller.

Time controller deactivated, sent the girl, along with a set of repair parameters. She discovered a small rectangular card. Through her eyes the image of the card was scanned and shunted into analysis. One nanosecond. Broken down into hexidecimal code, it flashed through perfect crystal memory storage as a beam of coherent light. There, deep in the core memory, listed under Gallifrey – cultural dynamics (symbols of). Two nanoseconds. The symbol was the seal of the Prydonion Chapter: Prydonion Chapter – politico-economic faction. Three nanoseconds. Renegade Time Lord, Ka Faraq Gatri, enemy of the Daleks, bringer of darkness.

The Doctor.

Four nanoseconds.

The Dalek Supreme felt a sudden thrill of fear.

The girl was back in the chair; the battle computer gestalt was running. The Dalek Supreme was getting tactical updates on the positions of its warriors, which were spread out in prepared defensive positions around the warehouse. The battle computer urged pursuit, capture and recorded disintegration of the Doctor. Five nanoseconds. Such an act would gain prestige with other renegade factions. Perhaps drawing them into the conflict with the Imperium. Six nanoseconds.

The Dalek Supreme gave the order to all renegade Daleks: *Seek, locate and exterminate the Doctor.*

Ace was following the Doctor, and the Doctor wasn't going to stop. A hundred metres behind them bits of brick were still falling onto the pavement. Two grey Daleks had opened fire from hiding, as Ace and the Doctor crossed the road. Ace hadn't seen the Doctor move when suddenly he swung her out of the line of fire. Brick-dust and flame erupted from the wall beside them.

The after-image of the energy bolt was still flashing on her retinas. 'They're eager,' was all the Doctor said.

Now the two Daleks chased them up the road.

They're not fast, thought Ace, but they keep on coming.

Ace pounded after the Doctor who ran light-footedly round a corner. They saw the Dalek before it saw them. Without looking the Doctor gripped Ace's arm and pivoted her around. Something blocked out the sky; she felt rough cloth against her cheek – a workman's tent. It went very quiet.

'Why didn't you just run off with the Hand of Omega and give it to the other Daleks?'

'With some luck,' said the Doctor, 'the imperial Daleks will eliminate the renegades for us. Besides, if I just roll up and give it to them, they'll get suspicious.'

'Suspicious of what?' asked Ace. 'You still haven't…' The Doctor placed a cool hand over her mouth and jerked his head to the left. Ace slowly turned her head and saw the rear of a grey Dalek half a metre from them. She closed her mouth and swallowed carefully.

Private Abbot saw Sergeant Smith motion with his arm and led the section out of the school gates. Abbot's grip on his gun was sweaty – he didn't have any faith in it any more, not even with the special-issue armour piercing rounds. Might as well spit at the damned pepperpots.

'All right,' said Smith, 'come with me, and keep your eyes peeled for Ace and the Doctor.'

Abbot glanced back at Bellos who carried the anti-tank rifle. 'Hey,' he whispered. 'If we see a pepperpot, do me a favour will you?'

Bellos grunted. 'What?'

'Don't miss,' said Abbot.

'Shut it,' hissed Smith.

I wonder what his beef is? thought Abbot. Adjusting his grip on the gun, he scuttled across the road.

Mike ran up to the pub window and checked inside. Nothing. Behind him the section was pressed warily into the pub wall. He waved Bellos and Amery into point on the intersection of the alley and Coal Hill Road. The two men quickly set up the launcher and slipped a round into the back. Amery crouched down and readied a second rocket.

It was quiet.

Mike was watching for Daleks, white and gold ones. Ratcliffe had assured him that the threat came from them. He felt a twinge of regret for Matthews and the others killed at Totters Lane, but Ratcliffe explained it so well – sacrifices had to be made.

Mike signalled Abbot forward. The soldier got into position behind a lamppost, gun at his shoulder and eyes alert to any movement. They were good lads. Once the Association was in power it would need men like that. Disciplined men who knew their jobs. Afterwards.

But first, Mike wanted to see Ace safe.

'Sarge,' called Abbot. 'Movement, up the alley.'

Mike slipped the safety off his gun.

The TARDIS was standing where they had left it in the shadow of the alley. Ace stared at the smooth blue paint on its surface. It was unnaturally smooth, that strange shade of blue. It was all she could do not to push open the door and go in.

'Couldn't we just…?' said Ace, nodding at the time-space machine.

'No,' said the Doctor. 'We've got work to do. Here comes the military.'

Ace looked and saw Mike running towards them a big grin on his face. 'Where have you been?'

'Dalek hunting,' said the Doctor. 'Now it's the other way round.'

Ace felt absurdly pleased at the impressed expression on Mike's face. Let's play this nice and cool, said a voice in her head. Play what? asked another, younger voice. This! said the first voice. Oh, said the young voice, *that.*

'Is Gilmore still at the school?' asked the Doctor.

Mike looked quickly at the Doctor. 'Yes.'

'Then we had better get back and soothe his troubled brow,' said the Doctor and marched off. Ace hardly noticed.

Mike wished that Ace wouldn't look at him like that. The girl was so intense, but that was all right – he liked that. Mike wondered whether she kissed with the same intensity.

You're never going to find out, he told himself, unless you get something going soon. Mike had been thinking of and discarding one chat-up line after another. What could anyone say to a girl who attacks Daleks with a baseball bat? It had to be neutral sounding, but unmistakable. Mike cleared his throat.

'Ace? When we're finished with this lot do you fancy going to the pictures?' For a terrible moment he thought she was going to laugh.

'You're confident,' she said. 'What's on?'

Mike's mind went blank. 'Don't know.'

'Doesn't matter,' said Ace, 'I've probably already seen it on television.'

Mike had about three seconds to try to figure that out before a bolt of superheated plasma blew away the wall behind him. They both ducked, heads jerking round to look for the enemy. Mike saw them first.

They were grey Daleks.

No, thought Mike, this can't be right. Ratcliffe said.

'Daleks!' He grabbed Ace's hand and together they ran for the school. There was a flash to the left: smoke vented from the rear of the rocket launcher. Mike felt the heat of the rocket exhaust as the missile streaked past. It detonated behind him as it hit something.

Bellos hung on to the launcher as Amery shoved another missile up the pipe. Three hundred yards up the alley a Dalek was brewing up nicely. Dense off-white smoke was obscuring any movement behind it. Amery patted him on the shoulder, the signal that the second missile was ready. Bellos squinted through the ratchet sight. He could see nothing through the smoke.

'Come on, you lovelies,' he murmured, 'let's be having you.'

'We've got to fall back,' said Amery.

The haze was lifting, and within it shapes moved like shadows. There! One was framed in the rectangular sight. Belloos squeezed the trigger. He saw the missile shoot away, red and white flame as it accelerated. It struck the Dalek between gunstick and manipulator.

'Gotcha!' hissed Bellos. He felt the familiar rush of triumph. More Daleks emerged from the smoke. 'Get another one in,' he called over his shoulder. Amery was yelling about pulling back. Bellos was turning towards him when the light smacked him into oblivion.

Abbot flinched backwards. For one nightmarish moment he could see every bone in Bellos's body. He reflexively closed his eyes, but it stayed as an after-image, white bones against the darkness. Abbot rolled to the left, scrambling to get his feet under him. Amery was screaming somewhere off to the left. Abbot got his eyes open in time to see a Dalek bearing down on him. He tried to get his gun up but he knew it was too late. The gunstick started to point towards him.

The eyepiece exploded in shards of silver, the roar of the submachine-gun in his ear deafened him. A hand grabbed his collar and yanked him backwards.

'Get under cover,' said Sergeant Mike Smith. 'Move it.'

White lightning flashed past his face. Abbot found his feet and ran.

From the shelter of the school gate Ace winced. The energy bolt shot past Mike's head, barely missing. Beside her a soldier was shaking violently, a white-knuckled grip on a rocket launcher. Mike was firing point-blank at the Dalek to little effect. Another Dalek was homing in on him.

'Give me that,' snarled Ace and grabbed the rocket–launcher from the soldier. Mike threw himself down, under the level of the first Dalek's gunstick and rolled, putting the creative between himself and the second Dalek. Ace brought up the launcher and squeezed the trigger.

Nothing happened.

Mike was trying to make his way back to the gateway, zigzagging sharply. The second Dalek glided sideways, turning to get a clear shot.

Ace disengaged the safety and fired.

The top of a post box exploded in a fountain of cast iron. Mike sprinted the last ten metres and threw himself through the gate. Through the smoke, Ace saw another squadron of Daleks forming up.

'Come on, Ace,' yelled Mike. 'We'll let the recoilless take care of them.' He took her hand and started to pull her away. Ace took a last look at the mass of Daleks approaching. Next time she would get the thing aimed properly before she fired. She ran towards the school with Mike.

Rachel dodged back as a squad of soldiers hammered through the foyer on their way to the playground. They seemed to flow round Gilmore who stood in the centre calmly giving orders. Allison was yelling into a radio microphone trying to make herself heard above the yells and bangs.

'Five round the back, sir,' said a young corporal, 'about twenty at the front. Kaufman isn't sure he can hold them.'

'Get back there and tell Kaufman he doesn't have any choice.' Gilmore turned to her. Rachel saw a wildness in his eyes. 'Where are they coming from?'

'I don't know,' she shouted.

There was a muffled crump from outside.

'That was the recoilless,' said Gilmore. 'Ye gods, they must be in the playground.'

Where is the Doctor? thought Rachel.

The doors at the end of the foyer flew open and the Doctor swept in. There was a flash behind him, another crump and whistle from the gun outside. Mike and Ace charged in after him. Ace's face was flushed, her eyes were glittering.

Gilmore turned on the Doctor. 'I trust your little jaunt was successful.'

'Moderately so,' the Doctor said calmly. 'I'm afraid we brought back some Daleks.'

Ace wiped her face with a handkerchief.

'I don't get it,' said Mike. 'They've got the Hand of Omega, why don't they just leave?'

Ace's hand froze, holding the handkerchief to her face. The Doctor turned and looked at Mike. He took a step towards him and looked into his eyes. 'How did you know that?' he asked quietly.

Ace turned to look at Mike, her face suddenly drained of colour.

'Ace told me,' Mike said desperately.

'You toerag,' Ace said softly, 'you dirty lying scumbag.' Her hand lashed out at his chest. Mike staggered back, more from the fury on her face than the blow. The Doctor caught Ace by the waist.

'It can wait, Ace!' he said.

Ace flailed with her arms, legs kicking uselessly as the Doctor lifted her off her feet.

'You're a dead scumbag,' she screamed at the cowering man as the Doctor inexorably pulled her towards the stairwell. Ace turned to Gilmore. 'He's a grass, a dirty stinking grass,' she wailed. 'He's been selling us out to the Daleks.'

Mike flinched at the hatred on Ace's face. The Doctor's eyes battered at his skull.

'What's going on?' asked Gilmore. 'What are they talking about, Sergeant?'

Mike had a sick feeling in his stomach. He was going to lose it all. 'I didn't know it was the Daleks,' Mike was sweating. How could he explain the loyalties that had pulled him to this position: about Ratcliffe and the Association; their plans for the future; his feelings for Ace?

Ace. Her eyes were burning. But the Doctor's eyes were hiding a deep sadness. Mike looked away – perhaps the Doctor would understand.

'I can explain everything,' he said.

The foyer door exploded.

12

SATURDAY, 15:42

The target planet filled half the monitor. The shuttle was low enough for the cloud patterns to sweep past underneath. Onboard the pilot fed a continuous update to the commander. The screen flared as the ionosphere bit at the heatshields. The modular cargo bays held warriors webbed into a restraint matrix, and in a special section, isolated from the other Daleks, was the Abomination.

The shuttle started to vibrate as it cut a swathe through the thickening atmosphere; the flaring spread to encompass the entire view. Communications were cut off as a layer of ionized air enveloped the shuttle. The spot temperature of the heatshields began to approach that of the sun's interior.

The shuttle fell towards London like a flaming torch. Eyes watched it fall.

On the roof of a house in Hampstead, an eye nestled in the gable next to the television aerial. A sign advertised tile repairs courtesy of George Ratcliffe and Co. Data flashed from a microwave transmitter to a relay point on a roof of a tower block in Hackney and from there to the warehouse in Shoreditch.

The battle computer was getting reports from hidden

sensors placed in strategic positions over the south-east of England. An object was penetrating the atmosphere on a powered trajectory.

Smoke was drifting up the stairwells. Allison felt explosions as vibrations through the floor. There were Daleks on the ground floor. She could hear men screaming.

'What was that, Fylingdales, over?' she shouted into the radio microphone. The operator at the other end kept on talking in a calm voice, inaudible over the battle. Allison took a deep breath. 'I'm not reading you Fylingdales.'

Ace ran past her, clutching a large bundle of something explosive close to her chest.

'Say again, over.' Again the maddeningly quiet voice, something about a radar contact.

The Doctor ran by.

'Repeat that,' asked Allison.

'Ace,' shouted the Doctor, 'careful with that.'

Fylingdales repeated the message. Allison missed the crucial bit when half the stairwell blew out.

That's it, decided Allison. 'Speak up,' she shouted, 'or I'll eviscerate you, over.'

Fylingdales spoke up.

Imperial shuttlecraft entering atmosphere, reported the battle computer.

The Dalek Supreme considered this.

We must defend the Hand of Omega, it decided, *withdraw all units. Suicide warriors to defensive positions – stand by for attack by imperial Daleks.*

The battle computer spat out optimum strategy options. Recalibrating the time controller would take time; they had to hold the imperial stormtroopers until they could escape.

After that, Time would belong to them.

The Doctor threw himself on Ace. They both went skidding along the corridor floor. Blaster fire stitched a pattern where Ace had been standing.

'Close,' said Ace.

'Stay down,' hissed the Doctor.

'This isn't part of the plan,' said Ace, 'is it?'

Another bang and a light fitting hissed overhead.

'That's very perceptive of you.'

Rachel crawled over to them; one lens of her glasses had cracked.

'Hallo, Rachel,' said the Doctor. 'Coping?'

'I've done this before.'

'Really, when?'

'Summer of 1940.'

'The Battle of Britain, wicked,' said Ace. 'What was it like?'

'Not now, Ace,' said the Doctor.

Gilmore walked over and looked down at them. 'You can get up now,' he said. 'The Daleks are withdrawing.'

Abbot cautiously poked up his head from behind the wall of sandbags. The Daleks had turned and were leaving the playground, one of the destroyed ones belching a black oily smoke. Abbot slipped down again and leant against the wall. Fumbling in his pocket he pulled out a crumpled packet of woodbines and extracted a cigarette. He found a box of matches in Faringdon's pocket and lit one. It was difficult to light the cigarette because his hands were shaking. Abbot took a deep drag, and looked over at Faringdon. The soldier was missing his head.

Quite suddenly, Abbot began to cry.

Ace stared out of the window in the chemistry lab. 'They're retreating, all of them,' she told the others. She leaned out of the window. 'Wimps!' she shouted.

Rachel stared at the girl in disbelief. What does it take to shake this child? What kind of future is it that produces children like that?

'Doctor,' she said, 'we've had a report of a radar contact.'

'On a re-entry curve from low orbit?'

'Yes.'

'That'll be an imperial Dalek shuttlecraft,' said the Doctor.

'They're not landing a spaceship here?' asked Gilmore.

There was a rumble like thunder overhead.

'Here?' said the Doctor. 'No. We're much too far from the main action.'

The rumble was getting louder. Fragments of glass began to vibrate on the workbenches.

'You're sure?' asked Rachel.

Ace was staring up at the sky. 'Whoa,' she said.

'Ace,' yelled the Doctor, 'get away from the window.'

Ace came scrambling over the benches to them. The

rumble grew until it filled the room. Something blotted out the light. Instinctively they all ducked under the nearest bench. The window blew in, splinters of wood and glass burying themselves in the walls. Superheated gas screamed into the classroom. The noise was unbearable.

Something huge and technological travelled past the window.

Rachel found herself face to face with the Doctor.

The noise cut out suddenly.

'Well?' she cried.

'I think I may have miscalculated,' said the Doctor.

13
SATURDAY, 15:50

There was the crunch of powdering concrete. The shuttle rocked once on its suspension before settling. The imperial shuttle commander ordered the main doors unsealed.

Two scouts raced out to take point position. Their onboard sensors swept the playground. There was battle damage. Preliminary data indicated conflict between renegade Dalek forces and native military personnel.

Warrior section one unshipped from the port-bow module and filed swiftly away from the shuttle. The shuttle commander cautiously deployed them in defensive positions. Once the immediate area was secure, sections two and three deployed as a phalanx.

Orbital intelligence indicated that the main renegade staging area was 3500 metres to the east; native resistance was expected to be minimal. The shuttle commander's tactical computer showed orbital images of the local conurbation. Three optimum routes were picked out in neon green.

The shuttle commander decided to use all three routes. Section one would travel north, section two would go by the direct central route and section three via the south. Section four would unship and with the Abomination maintain perimeter defence. Its orders were rapidly downloaded into the warriors and scouts.

With only the faint whine from the scouts' overpowered motivators the imperial Dalek assault squad moved off.

Gilmore got to his feet and ran to the window. Glass crunched under his feet; tendrils of acrid smoke wound round his legs. Most of the window frame had been blasted inwards by…

Gilmore wanted to turn away from the window, turn around and walk away from what he suspected he would see. It took so much of himself to stare down into the playground.

It was dirty white, constructed from a series of polygons, it was ugly and it was large. Daleks in cream and gold livery moved around down there. Gilmore stepped back from the window.

'Right,' he said to the others, 'out of here, downstairs.'

Rachel, Ace and Allison went scrambling for the door. The Doctor remained where he was.

'Is that the mothership?' asked Gilmore.

'No,' said the Doctor, 'that's a shuttle. The mothership is much larger. Are you willing to co-operate with me?'

'Do I have a choice?'

'Well,' said the Doctor, 'you could go out there and make a gloriously futile gesture.'

'What do we do?'

'A little bit of piracy.'

Ace's shoulder hurt – a knot of tension in her back that refused to go away. She tried rotating the joint as she followed Rachel and Allison into the foyer.

'Ace,' said Mike from behind her.

'Go away,' she said, without turning round.

She felt him come closer. 'I didn't know about the Daleks,' he said. 'I was just doing Mr Ratcliffe a favour.'

'Do me a favour,' said Ace, 'and drown yourself.'

She wanted him gone before he saw the wetness in her eyes, but he wouldn't shut up. 'I just thought it was the right thing. Mr Ratcliffe had plans, such great plans.'

'Shut up.'

'I never really hated anyone. It's just that you have to look after your own…'

A smell invaded her nostrils, acrid, like…

'Keep the outsiders out…'

Hospital smell and…

'… just so your own people can get a fair crack.'

Disinfectant and charred wood.

Ace was facing him before she knew she had turned. Her hands were striking out at his chest, pushing him away.

'I said shut up!' she screamed. 'You betrayed the Doctor, you betrayed me. I trusted you – I even liked you – and all the time…'

Ace turned her back on him, she couldn't look at him any more. Her shoulder hurt. On the table in front of her was a stack of metal boxes. 'Danger, High Explosives' was stencilled along their sides, in yellow letters. She reached out for the top box.

'Sergeant Smith.' It was Gilmore.

Mike mumbled something in reply.

'Attention!' Gilmore shouted at parade ground volume.

Ace's hand faltered on its way to the box. She turned to look back.

Mike stood rigidly to attention. Group Captain Gilmore was beside him, face impassive. Behind the group captain stood an armed corporal.

'Sergeant Smith,' said Gilmore, 'I am placing you under close arrest under suspicion of offences contrary to the Official Secrets Act.' The corporal moved forward. 'You will surrender your weapon.'

Mike handed over his submachine-gun.

'Dismissed.'

Mike's salute was crisp and formal, but Gilmore ignored it. Mike turned and followed the corporal out. Ace could see pain on the group captain's face and then she too looked away.

Imperial scout Dalek seven shot down the street at thirty kilometres an hour. Its overpowered motor lifted its fairing two centimetres above the primitive road surface. Sensor signals fanned out from the bulb housings on its torso. The creature inside rushed headlong through a world of enhanced sensory impression.

Three metres behind and left, scout eight ran back-up position.

They were eight minutes out from the landing zone, clearing the central route for the warriors of section two. The street terminated in a T-junction. Blue light flashed at the Dalek's base as scout seven increased power to the motor and skipped the curb, crabbing sideways as the engine strained to compensate for the ninety degree turn to the right. There was a noisy electronic protest as the engineering controls red-lined.

Scout eight took the corner more sedately, pirouetting to cover the left-hand street with its gunstick. Scout seven wound down the power and scanned the area ahead. The street was clear of life or power emissions. Ahead it ran under a bridge, creating a long lightless tunnel.

Scout seven raised the shuttle commander on the VHF link. Scout seven reporting – area 25 – 09 clear.

Shifting its vision to infra-red, scout seven moved forward.

In the darkness the renegade warriors were waiting. They were veteran campaigners, their battle computers old with experience. Every stratagem, every tactic learned on a thousand worlds was captured in prisms of crystal.

Now they waited, powered down, with baffles deployed to mask their emission signature. Remote sensors deployed in the street beyond the tunnel pinpointed the position of the approaching imperial scouts and fed data to the warriors' fire control units.

Their orders were to hold off the imperial Daleks, even at the cost of their own destruction. They would do this thing and sacrifice themselves without question.

They were Daleks.

The attack came as a blizzard of electromagnetic static. Electronic countermeasures pods twinned with the remote sensors attacked scout seven through its sensor pods. The wave of static crashed over the sensitive instruments causing feedback to lash up the data bus and into the Dalek proper. Scout seven went blind in a microsecond. At the same time, machine code instructions hidden inside the random noise laid siege to the processors that regulated the Dalek's life support. The internal systems fought back, defence subroutines attempted to locate the intruder program and eliminate it. They failed. The program was in. From that moment on scout seven began to die. Rogue commands from the intruder program voided food and waste tanks into the life chamber. The creature inside drowned.

The blaster bolt that blew away its top half was little more than a coup de grâce.

The imperial Dalek shuttle commander checked the updates on the fighting. Advance scouts had encountered renegade warriors in prepared positions. Battle projections indicated that both the northern and southern routes would be costly to force. The central route was equally well defended, but was the shortest to the renegade base.

The shuttle commander reached a decision. Sections one and three would attack along the north and south flanks as planned. Section two was to clear the preliminary positions on the centre, while section four moved into position for a final assault. The Abomination would be held in reserve.

The shuttle commander issued its orders over the command net. Section four formed into an attack phalanx behind it and moved out.

*

The Doctor watched from the chemistry lab as the remaining Daleks in the playground filed out. As opponents, the Daleks were nothing if not predictable.

He heard Gilmore come through the door behind him.

'The imperial Daleks appear to have committed their entire force,' said the Doctor.

'Meaning?' asked Gilmore.

'There's only a skeleton crew left on board.'

'They're very confident.'

'Too confident,' said the Doctor. 'It's a Dalek weakness.'

Gilmore turned to go.

'Group Captain?' called the Doctor.

'Yes?'

'Thank you for co-operating.'

Gilmore looked at the Doctor, his eyes were bleak.

'Only a fool argues with his Doctor,' he said.

14
SATURDAY, 16:05

Section one on the northern route engaged the enemy first. The renegade warriors were dug in at the end of a broad road flanked by residential housing.

Scouts one and two had reported that the terrain on either side was impassable. The only possible tactic open to the imperial Daleks of section one was a frontal assault. They went in *Cach-ya Beng*, the six finger formation – three pairs, forward Dalek and back-up. The forward Daleks maintained a steady fire on the renegade warriors while each back-up Dalek strove to locate and eliminate the ECM pods hidden along the road.

The exchange of fire was swift and vicious. In the first attack section one lost three Daleks, and the renegades suffered only superficial damage. The imperial Daleks retreated quickly laying down a covering pattern of blaster fire.

Three columns of greasy black smoke boiled into the sky.

But all the ECM pods had been destroyed.

Both Dalek factions settled into inconclusive sniping fire along the length of the road. Battle updates flashed through the command-net to the shuttle commander.

*

The Doctor watched Ace. The young woman stood unmoving in the school foyer. Around her soldiers continued to clear up the mess left from the battle.

A body was pulled from the rubble by the stairwell. A medic knelt by him and put his hand on the man's throat. The medic looked up and shook his head. Stretcher bearers moved in to take the corpse. The Doctor wondered who the dead man had been, whether he was married, had children.

The Doctor looked at Ace again. Her eyes were glazed, her lips parted slightly. He could see her chest fall and rise in rapid shallow breathing.

She's no good to me like this, decided the Doctor and started towards her.

'Ace?' he said. Her head turned slowly, a lost look in her eyes. 'I don't suppose you're interested in a misguided attack on a Dalek shuttle.' Ace merely stared at his face. 'Suicidal, of course.' There, a flicker of interest. 'No, I'll just have to do it myself.'

The Doctor walked away, just slowly enough.

'Oi!' Ace was suddenly at his side. 'Wait a minute.'

The Doctor smiled, inside, where it wouldn't show.

Allison had never seen Rachel this angry.

'Out of my way, Group Captain,' she shouted, jabbing a finger at Gilmore's chin. 'Or I may do something unscientific to your face.'

Gilmore retreated a step and banged into the foyer doors. 'Professor Jensen, 1 cannot allow you to…'

'Allow me to what?' yelled Rachel, forcing Gilmore back through the double doors. 'I'm sick of your regulations, rules and restrictions. If I want to put myself in danger, that's my concern.'

Allison could see Ace and the Doctor standing in the foyer, watching them. Ace was grinning. Allison caught her eye and gave an embarrassed shrug.

Rachel saw the Doctor. She pushed past Gilmore and marched up to the Doctor. 'We're coming with you,' she told him, 'whatever this martinet says. I'm not going to spend the rest of my life wondering what was going on. I'm going to find out, even if it means following you into the jaws of hell itself.'

'It's very dangerous,' said the Doctor.

'So is ignorance,' said Rachel.

15
SATURDAY, 16:11

The southern route.

Section three was pulling back in disarray. It had hit the renegade Daleks in one glorious charge. The renegades met them with a solid line of blaster fire. The first wave dissolved under its intensity, expanding globes of shattered polycarbide and soft Dalek flesh. The second wave of imperial Daleks had pressed on, blasters probing for the elusive enemy. Two renegades had been destroyed before the section had been forced to withdraw.

Tactical updates flashed through the command-net. The imperial shuttle commander relayed the communiques through its uplink to the main computer on the mothership. The main computer chewed up the data in moments and tactical options flashed down to the shuttle commander.

The shuttle commander ordered section four to form up behind the Abomination. In three minutes they would reach reserve positions behind section two.

The attacks on the northern and southern routes had served their purpose. Renegade defence tactics had been challenged and the responses analysed. The attack on their central positions could start as soon as the reserves were in position.

Sections one and two would continue to pin down the flanks.

Section two, ordered the shuttle commander, *prepare to attack.*

Rachel stared at the rope in her hands, forcing her mind back to the 1930s and Hawthorne's voice. The mouse goes through the hole. Rachel tied the rope around the leg of the bench.

The Doctor stood on the window sill with the other end of the rope. Allison and Ace stood watching as he tied an expert lasso.

The mouse runs round the tree and nips back through the hole, Rachel could hear Hawthorne's voice, almost smell the grass and the coal fires. 'What happens next?' asked the eight-year-old Rachel. Hawthorne laughed. Then the mouse comes out, and a bird gets it. Rachel pulled the rope tight and snapped back to the present day. The shattered chemistry lab, an alien spacecraft and the presence of evil.

She checked the knot, it was secure. Thank God for the Girl Guides, thought Rachel and stood up. Gilmore was looking at her.

'Why are we doing this?' asked Allison.

'Elementary piracy,' said the Doctor. 'Dalek shuttles have massive ground defences, sophisticated anti-aircraft weapons, and an unguarded service hatch on the top.' He looked at them and smiled. 'Once I'm down, I'll attempt to open the hatch. Ace, you come down after me, then Gilmore, followed by Rachel and Allison, any questions?'

Yes, thought Rachel. Why am I doing this?

'No,' said the Doctor and threw the lasso.

The lasso whistled out and slipped around one of the shuttle's antennas.

So what if I was aiming at the other antenna? thought the Doctor as he pulled the rope tight. This will do just as well. He hooked the handle of his umbrella over the rope and pushed off.

The rope sang as he left the window and sped down towards the shuttle. The sky was blue; in the distance he could hear the sound of Daleks killing each other. He landed on the shuttle's roof as silently as a cat.

He found the service hatch. The locking mechanism was an eight digit code based on a prime number in the sigma series. It took him a couple of seconds to crack. There was a muffled thump as the interlocking electromagnetic fields disengaged. The hatch dropped inwards by three centimetres and slid open.

The Doctor swung over and dropped into the dim interior.

He landed on the deck and paused. He was in a short access corridor. Glow-plates mounted on the bulkhead cast a ruddy light over pipes and cables. There was the smell of carbon lubricant.

Something scuttled away from his feet.

The Doctor's head jerked round to the direction of the noise. A little servo-robot climbed halfway up the sloping bulkhead and stoped, watching him with tiny red LED eyes. The Doctor scowled and the servo-robot vanished into a vent.

The Doctor crept to the forward bulkhead door and stamped on the pressure pad on the deck. The door whispered open and the Doctor rushed onto the bridge.

The shuttle pilot was instantly aware of him.

'Hallo,' said the Doctor.

The shuttle pilot was locked into its control position. Its eyepiece twisted impotently to follow the Doctor as he advanced.

'Emergency, emergency,' screamed the Dalek. The Doctor jammed the point of his umbrella into the control console. A panel opened and flux circuits spilled out. The Doctor jabbed again and crystal shattered. The shuttle pilot was suddenly isolated from the command-net.

'Human on the bridge,' screamed the Dalek, unaware that only the Doctor could hear it.

'I'm not human,' said the Doctor and started sorting through the circuits. Cables snaked through his fingers with an unpleasant movement of their own.

'You are the Doctor,' said the Dalek. 'You are the enemy of the Daleks.'

'Yes,' said the Doctor, and with a sharp pull of his right hand blew every circuit in the Dalek. The shuttle pilot shuddered violently for a second. Its eyepiece flailed around then slumped down. A wisp of smoke drifted up from its dome.

'Goodbye,' said the Doctor.

16
SATURDAY, 16: 15

Scan-op tasted a new energy pattern emanating from the renegade base. The configuration was unmistakable: it was the primary starting field of a time controller. Scan-op passed the data on to the systems controller, who informed the Emperor.

The renegade's time corridor is being primed.

Estimated time to its operation? asked the Emperor.

Estimated at thirty-one minutes, replied the systems controller.

The Emperor quickly reviewed the tactical situation on the planet below. He felt apprehensive – it was going to be close. The imperial Daleks were forming up for their offensive, but when they broke through they would still have to fight 1500 metres to the renegade base. They must secure the Hand of Omega before the renegades could vanish back to their own time. He had not made all these sacrifices to be thwarted now.

Inform the shuttle commander of the deadline. The Emperor's thoughts tasted of suppressed anger. *Failure will not be tolerated,* it added.

The imperial shuttle commander felt the shuttle pilot link go dead. It considered sending a warrior back to the shuttle to investigate but the Emperor's orders overrode it. The shuttle commander was drawing data from scout eight. A synthesis of data from orbital cameras, and the scout's own sensors resolved into a three-dimensional situation map. The tunnel was a tracery of green; estimated positions of the renegade warriors were fuzzy grey blobs. ECM pods were silver dots sprinkling the killing zone at the tunnel's mouth. Section two showed up as a phalanx of hard-edged white diamonds. Three hundred metres behind section two, more diamonds marked section four's position – the Abomination was a single red star at their centre.

Section two advance, ordered the shuttle-commander, *for the glory of the Emperor and the* Ven-Katri Davrett.

The girl was the battle computer; the battle computer was the girl. Locked into symbiosis they fed the tactical situation to the Dalek Supreme.

The Dalek Supreme felt the imperial Daleks start their attack. Strange, alien emotions were creating problems for its life support systems. The girl's feelings were bleeding through the gestalt interface into the Dalek Supreme. She was playing. Each tactical problem thrown up by the battle computer was a game to her. Guided by the two thousand years of experience stored in the data banks she was solving them, each solution triggering a shot of energy to the pleasure centres in her brain.

The girl was having *fun.*

For one vertiginous moment the Dalek Supreme wanted to skip.

*

Section two advanced towards the shadows that hid the mouth of the tunnel. They moved slowly, their power plants generating a complex overlapping pattern of sensor waves.

The remains of scout seven marked the range of the renegade ECM pods. The imperial Daleks switched to infra-red, eyesticks hunting for targets. As they passed scout seven the ECM attack began. This time the waves of static hit the sensor wave pattern put out by the imperial Daleks. The method of ECM attack had been studied and analysed during the costly attacks on the northern and southern routes. This time the imperial Daleks were ready.

The silent electronic battle continued as section two advanced. The harmonics created by the conflict of sensor wave against sensor wave caused the nitrogen molecules in the atmosphere to vibrate faster. The air around the imperial Daleks began to shimmer with heat. They continued to advance.

A blaster bolt flashed out from the renegade positions. It struck the lead imperial just below its gunstick. The superheated plasma punched a fist-sized hole through the armour, ripped into the Dalek's innards and exploded. For a moment the top casing contained a fireball as hot as a hydrogen bomb. Then the top of the Dalek vanished in a burst of light.

The remaining imperial Daleks zeroed in on the place where the attack had originated.

On the shuttle commander's situation map, one of the grey blobs sharpened to a hard point. Exterminate, ordered the shuttle commander, *now*!

Five gunsticks jerked into position. Computer-enhanced vision locked on to the shadows of an alcove near the end of the tunnel. Five tiny parcels of death, the air screaming in their wake, raced away from the imperial Daleks.

The renegade warrior saw the incoming bolts. With a convulsive burst of its motor it vainly tried to shift out of danger. The first bolt smashed away the wall that had sheltered the Dalek, the rest smacked into its body. The renegade went spinning backwards, breaking up into flaming pieces as it went.

The grey diamond on the situation map winked out. The shuttle commander noted that the grey blobs marking estimated renegade positions were beginning to move. Each movement gave away a renegade's exact position. This was according to plan.

A renegade warrior shot across the far end of the tunnel. The imperial Daleks immediately tracked it, again laying down the co-ordinated fire that had been so devastating before.

While their attention was occupied by the first renegade, however, two grey Daleks slipped sideways into position and fired. A glancing hit immobilized one imperial; another was hit just below its comm-light and exploded. The two renegades slipped out of sight before the imperial Daleks could respond.

The Dalek Supreme was fighting another bout of disorientation. Its normally sluggish heartbeat was speeding past safety parameters. Its life support computer was administering greater and greater doses of tranquillizers in an effort to compensate. The drugs made it hard for the Dalek Supreme to concentrate, and it was forced to leave the conduct of the battle to the girl and the battle computer.

The central front was weakening and the entire renegade reserve of six warriors had been ordered in to strengthen it. The girl, wrapped in her cocoon of data and warm electronic pleasure, smiled. Even if the imperials committed all their remaining Daleks they would never reach the warehouse in time to stop the renegades' escape.

The Emperor watched as the last white diamond on the situation map blinked once and vanished.

Section two has been annihilated, reported the systems co-ordinator. *The shuttle commander is planning to commit the reserves.*

Estimated time before renegade time corridor established? asked the Emperor.

Twenty minutes, reported Scan-op.

The Emperor checked the situation map. Fools. Even with the reserves there was little chance of punching through the renegade defences before their time corridor was established. I made them cunning, it thought, but also too rigid. The shuttle commander has the perfect weapon but will not use it. That is why I am Emperor.

The Emperor opened a direct channel to the shuttle commander. *Move the special weapons Dalek into position,* it transmitted.

*

Mike stared at the Formica top of the table. Facing him across its cracked and stained surface sat Corporal Grant. A fifty watt bulb cast gigantic shadows off the boiler and the broken Dalek transmat. The cellar smelt of old iron and damp wood.

Mike wanted to understand the hatred in Ace's eyes. There was a bruise on his chest where she had struck him. Mike was sure Ace would have tried to kill him if he had provoked her further. He had seen that look once before, in Singapore. Mike had been on the last dregs of a twenty-four hour pass in some nameless bar in the red light district. Fans churned the sluggish air around the room as he spent his money on the local beer and eyed up the talent. The pale faces of the soldiers were slick with sweat.

The fight started suddenly. A bottle shattered; a big sailor staggered back roaring, one hand clutching his shoulder. Blood welled from between his fingers. There was a struggle at the end of the bar – three Navy ratings were trying to restrain a fourth. He was a small sailor with a ferret-like face. Clutching a broken bottle, he fought to be free of the other men.

The big sailor looked stupidly at the blood on his hand, and then at the ferret-faced sailor. The big sailor swore and lurched forward, cocking his red-stained fist. The smaller man struggled in silence, lips pulled back to show his teeth. Then Mike saw his eyes. They were bright with violence; Mike knew that the big sailor was going to die.

He was saved by the Chinese barman who leaped over the bar and waved a meat cleaver at both men. The sailor with the ferret face was dragged from the bar by his friends; the big sailor backed away from the barman, hands raised in a placatory gesture. The barman lowered his meat cleaver and went back behind the bar. It was the barman's eyes that reminded Mike of Ace's — they had showed vehemence and contempt in equal measure.

Why did she look at me as if I were rubbish? Mike wanted some answers.

'Tea?' asked Corporal Grant.

'Yeah,' said Mike, 'thanks.'

Grant pushed his chair away from the table. Mike watched him as he got up. The corporal, like all professional soldiers, had his tea-making gear stashed nearby. As Grant turned and walked to the corner of the cellar Mike stood up and stepped away from the table. His chair scraped against the floor, and alerted by the sound Grant turned and said: 'Come on, Sarge.'

It was funny that Grant knew what Mike intended, before he knew himself.

Grant went for his pistol, but Mike got to him first.

Rachel was dizzy from sliding down the rope. She tried to look round as Gilmore hustled her through a hatchway, but it was all a dark blur. She touched the doorframe as she stepped through. The metal had a weird texture, almost like plastic. Rachel sniffed her fingers and gingerly tasted one with her tongue. It tasted tinny.

Inside the next chamber was a Dalek, set into a podium. The Doctor was beside it, holding a long thin tube. Rachel recognized it as a Dalek manipulator arm.

Ace was tapping the inert Dalek with her forefinger.

'What did you do to it?' she asked the Doctor.

'I short-circuited it,' said the Doctor. He turned to look at Rachel. 'Daleks are such boring conversationalists.'

Rachel looked around. Bulkheads of the strange metal sloped inwards, the ceiling was bare and of the same metal. Apart from the Dalek and what she assumed was a control podium, there were no other fittings.

'I can't see any controls,' said Rachel.

'What would a Dalek do with a switch?' said the Doctor.

He slotted the plunger end of the manipulator arm into a shallow depression in the side of the control podium. 'The Daleks plug in direct.'

The Doctor twisted the arm. There was a series of clicks and the plunger was locked in. The Doctor started to sort through the fine cables that hung out of the free end of the manipulator arm.

'It's very functional,' said Allison.

'Daleks are not known for their aesthetic sense,' said the Doctor. He made an adjustment to the wires. There was a low hum. A wide rectangle of light formed in front of the inert Dalek, hanging in space two inches from the front bulkhead.

A television picture, thought Rachel, projected on to thin air. Rachel remembered the extruded glass fibre cables they found in the destroyed Daleks. She had a sudden vision of bursts of coherent light carrying digitized information at the speed of light. A picture built up of digital information, spat out of an electron gun. No, not an electron gun, she realized, a light-maser through a flat prism decoded into the thin air. Gods, a three-dimensional image.

Rachel snapped out of her thoughts to find the Doctor had turned his head towards her. His eyes were grey and intense. Rachel felt them peeling away her face, looking into her mind.

'No,' said the Doctor, 'not for twenty years.'

Rachel blinked. The Doctor had his back to her, working on the manipulator arm. Rachel shook her head to clear it.

'Now,' said the Doctor, 'let's see if we can find out just what they are up to.'

The screen flickered, a grid of white lines formed. Bright points of light scattered across the picture, tiny symbols in red and green labelled them.

A starmap, decided Rachel.

The Doctor made some more adjustments and different patterns formed – a blue and green planet symbol. It was the Earth. Now a complex pattern of short, angular arrows wove its way through the starmap. 'What are those?' asked Rachel.

'Four-dimensional vectors,' said the Doctor. 'They mark the path the imperial Dalek mothership will take.' He pointed to a cluster of lines. 'See, they're shifting to compensate for the Earth's orbital shift and the passing of time – I did mention that these Daleks can travel in time.'

'Yeah,' said Ace, 'but it's very crude and nasty.'

She's doing it again, thought Rachel, I hate it when she does that.

'That's the Earth,' said the Doctor, pointing. 'That must be the time corridor that connects it to another system.' The screen jumped, different stars again. This time the vectors pointed inwards, towards an orange star at the centre of the screen.

'The planet Skaro,' said the Doctor. His voice was suddenly soft. 'So, the Daleks have returned to their ancestral seat.'

The Dalek was insane. Radiation had altered the structure of its mind and made it mad. The mark of its insanity was, that of all Daleks in the great race of Daleks, it had a name.

It was called the Abomination.

They had given it another name: in the imperial battle roster it was listed as the special weapons Dalek.

The Emperor had decreed its creation.

They had ripped it from its birthing cradle, aware like all Daleks. They had taken it and placed it in its shell and given it functions. But the shell they gave it was wrong, twisted, a single function monstrosity – a vast weapon and the power plant to drive it. They led it to the firing range and had it destroy to order. As it fired, the first backwash of radiation sleeted through its fragile body.

It served in many campaigns: *Pa Jass-Gutrik*, the war of vengeance against the Movellans; *Pa Jaski-Thal*, the liquidation war against the Thals; and *Pa Jass-Vortan*, the time campaign – the war to end all wars.

Every time it fought, the radiation from its pulse gun saturated its life support chamber. Chromosomes altered shape, its vestigial pituitary gland became active and hormones chased unfettered through its bloodstream. It became changed, twisted and insane. It committed the blasphemy of knowing who it was.

The other Daleks feared it for its sense of self and for its name. They would have destroyed it. Only the will of the Emperor kept it alive.

The shuttle commander activated the special command circuit. The Abomination's mind came alive with data. The situation map flashed into its forebrain. Designated targets were staked out in yellow.

The power plant ran up to full operation. Slowly the two-tonne bulk of the special weapons Dalek rose off the road surface. Section four formed up behind it. The command net channelled their sensor readings directly into the situation map.

The special weapons Dalek turned the corner and moved on towards the tunnel mouth. Target renegade warriors showed up as pink blobs as sensors homed in on their heat emissions.

At forty metres range, two renegade Daleks broke cover and cut across the far end of the tunnel. The special weapons Dalek's scopes pinned them in digital crosswires. A fire was lit in the belly of the Abomination.

At thirty metres range the special weapons Dalek halted. Its huge gun twisted in its mount. The fire in its belly erupted and was spat out the barrel at the renegade Daleks.

In a single instant the two Daleks boiled away into the atmosphere. The concussion rocked the special weapons Dalek backwards. Then it drove on, seeking new targets.

That is why, thought the special weapons Dalek, they call me the Abomination.

*

'We've seen enough,' said the Doctor. 'Time to leave.'

Amen to that, thought Rachel.

'Stand back,' said the Doctor. He did something devious to the manipulator arm. A section of the floor slid away to reveal a shaft. Vapour wafted upwards. Rachel could hear an intermittent hiss coming from somewhere close. The Doctor looked at Allison. 'Jump,' he said.

Allison looked down the shaft. 'What about the massive ground defences?'

'Oh,' said the Doctor, 'I've turned those off.'

Allison jumped; there was a thump from below. 'It's all right,' she called up, 'there's something soft down here.'

'After you, Group Captain,' said Rachel.

Gilmore started to climb cautiously down into the shaft. 'Thank you, Professor Jensen,' said Gilmore before he disappeared.

Rachel heard the hissing sound again, then it stopped. There was a rattle of ball-bearings. Rachel checked the shaft again.

'Ace,' said the Doctor, 'time to go.' He looked around. 'Ace?'

'Coming, Professor,' said Ace.

Rachel looked up as Ace came over and saw her slipping something into her rucksack. Behind Ace, paint had been sprayed on the rear bulkhead: 'Ace woz' ere in 63.'

Rachel closed her eyes and jumped into the shaft.

Ace landed on a soft spongy surface. She reached down and touched the floor. It felt like packing foam.

'This way,' hissed Rachel from the darkness. Ace followed her voice. There was a glimmer of light from in front. Ace saw that they were in a short hexagonal corridor about twenty metres long. Rectangular archways left and right opened into dark empty spaces. More of the packing material was strewn on the floor.

'Where's the Doctor?' asked Gilmore.

'Here I am.'

Ace jumped at his voice – she hadn't heard him come down the shaft.

'I can't get the door open,' said Gilmore.

The Doctor squeezed past Ace, Rachel and Allison to where Gilmore was pushing at the hatch. The Doctor checked the floor and then stamped hard on one particular spot. There was a sharp hiss of hydraulics and the hatch swung open. Daylight poured in. Gilmore drew his service revolver and stepped out. They all bundled out behind him. Ace blinked in the light.

Gilmore holstered his revolver. 'Playground's clear.' He started off towards the school. Rachel and Allison followed.

'I rigged a communications relay into the shuttle control systems,' said the Doctor. 'We can monitor the Daleks with the transmat in the cellar.'

'You can't do that,' said Ace, 'you mashed up the transmat.'

'I,' said the Doctor, 'can do anything I like.'

Rachel watched the soldiers scatter as Gilmore strode through the school foyer.

He hasn't changed, thought Rachel.

A soldier lurched into her and she almost fell. The man staggered on a few paces clutching his head. He looked as if he was going to collapse.

'Allison,' called Rachel. She caught up with the man and grabbed his shoulders as he collapsed. Allison arrived to help Rachel just in time to stop the soldier falling.

'It's Corporal Grant,' said Allison. She gently prised away the Corporal's hand and felt his skull.

Rachel spotted Gilmore talking to a couple of men down the hall. 'Group Captain,' she called. Still Gilmore did not turn. 'Ian!' she shouted. Gilmore's head snapped round.

'What happened?' Allison asked the corporal.

'Sergeant Smith,' said the corporal, his words were slurred.

Concussion? wondered Rachel.

Gilmore arrived and put his weight under the man. 'Is he all right?' he asked Allison.

'No idea,' said Allison, 'I'm a physicist.'

A cool hand brushed Rachel's hand aside. It was the Doctor. He checked the corporal's pupils and then the pulse at his throat. Then he reached out and tweaked one of the corporal's earlobes.

'He'll be fine,' said the Doctor. 'Rachel and Allison, I'll need your help.'

'Sorry?' said Rachel.

The corporal shook his head; his legs steadied and this took his own weight.

Rachel stepped back as the man straightened. When she looked for the Doctor he had gone.

'What did he say?' she asked Allison.

'He said he needed our help.'

'That's what I thought he said.'

'He's got my pistol,' said the corporal.

'Allison,' said Rachel, 'get your hands off that man's scalp and come on.'

Now, thought Rachel, the Doctor wants my help.

Mike crept closer to the open gates. Ratcliffe's warehouse looked quiet, but Mike knew better than that.

The sound of another explosion came from the south east; columns of smoke drifted up above the skyline.

He checked the pistol and tucked it into the waist of his trousers. He had been forced to abandon the Ford Prefect half a mile back because of the fight between the Daleks. In the end, he sneaked through a derelict house to get past.

Mike walked through the gates and stopped: the yard was deserted. He started towards the sliding doors at the end of the yard. Then he saw it, tucked away in the far left corner and mounted on trestles. It was the coffin that the Doctor had buried. Mike realized that this was the Hand of Omega.

Mike went cold. They wouldn't leave that unguarded, he thought.

He spun round and found himself facing two Daleks. They were in grey and black livery – the Daleks that the Doctor called renegades. Mike quickly put up his hands. He saw their gunsticks take aim.

'No,' he shouted desperately. 'No, don't. I have a message for Mr Ratcliffe.' He didn't know if they had understood, but they didn't fire. 'A message for Mr Ratcliffe,' he repeated. The Daleks moved forward; Mike expected to die.

'You are my prisoner,' said the Dalek, and Mike relaxed. 'You will obey all instructions or you will be exterminated.'

'You said it, mate.'

'Watch your end,' said Allison. Rachel tried to get a better grip on the big television set – it kept threatening to slip out of her hands. They started down the cellar stairs again.

'When the Doctor said he needed our help,' said Rachel, 'I hoped he meant more in the technical area.'

'It was a vain hope,' said Allison.

The Doctor and Ace were by the transmat. The Doctor had pulled the panelling off the shattered consoles and was buried in a spray of cables. When Ace saw Rachel and Allison coming down the stairs with the television, she tapped him on the shoulder.

The Doctor pulled his head out of the console and smiled at them. 'Good, you got it,' he said. 'Put it down on here.' He patted the transmat dais.

Rachel and Allison heaved the television on to the dais. The Doctor immediately started running cables from the transmat to the television.

Allison watched in fascination. 'How does he do that?'

'Do what?' asked Ace.

'It's easy,' said the Doctor, 'when you've had nine hundred years' experience.'

Nine hundred years, thought Rachel, right. She

watched the Doctor's fingers working. Precisely what he did, Rachel couldn't make out, but under his hands grew a complicated assembly that ran from transmat to television.

'The Daleks got themselves in a war with the Movellans,' said the Doctor, 'who are a race of androids. They're just as nasty as the Daleks but more attractive to look at. The Movellans decimated the Dalek battle order with a selective virus.'

He's not even looking at what he's doing, realized Rachel. How does he do it? Is it instinct?

'Am I boring you?' asked the Doctor.

Allison's eyes had a glazed look. Ace was grinning.

Rachel shook her head, and the Doctor smiled.

'The virus fragmented the Daleks and left them in isolated factions, one of which seems to have resettled Skaro. This imperial faction seems to be in conflict with a force of renegade Daleks.' The Doctor stopped working and looked up at Rachel. 'And that's odd.'

'What's odd about some internecine violence?' said Rachel. 'There's been enough of it on this planet.'

'Daleks don't have internecine conflicts,' said the Doctor, shaking his head. 'One Dalek meets another Dalek, they bang databases, and one winds up giving orders to the other, except…'

'Except what?'

'Except,' said Ace, 'when one Dalek doesn't recognize another Dalek as being a Dalek.'

The Doctor and Rachel both looked at Ace. 'Very good, Ace,' said the Doctor. 'How did you come to that?'

Ace grinned. 'Simple, ain't it. Renegade Daleks are

blobs. Imperial Daleks aren't blobs – they're bionic blobs with bits added. You can tell Daleks are into racial purity, so one faction of Daleks reckons that the other blobs are too different, mutants, not pure in their blobbiness any more.'

'Result?'

'They hate each others' chromosomes,' said Ace. 'War to the death.'

'With us in the middle,' said Allison.

The Doctor pulled a slim case from his pocket. He pushed a switch on the side and it clicked open. A lens and body assembly snapped out. The Doctor attached another cable to it and placed it carefully on top of the television.

'Now, Ace,' said the Doctor, 'let's see which blobs are winning.'

Mike carefully watched the Black Dalek. It moved silently through Ratcliffe's office and stopped by the desk. There, a young girl was bent over a globe; inside the globe, lightning flared.

The two Daleks had ordered him into the office. Ratcliffe was waiting there on his knees.

The Black Dalek – the Dalek Supreme – turned its eyestick to regard him. 'Kneel,' it had ordered, and Mike had knelt. Then that creepy little girl had come in and started working on the globe.

'Repairs to the time controller complete,' said the girl.

'Prepare to leave,' ordered the Black Dalek.

Ratcliffe nudged Mike with his elbow. 'Without that thing,' he whispered, 'they're stuck here. A man in possession of that would have something to bargain with.'

'For what? Our lives?'

'Nothing so mundane. If we had that, we could demand anything.'

'You never give up, do you?'

Ratcliffe chuckled. 'That's what separates us from animals and the sub-human – we never give up.' He leaned closer to Mike. 'But we must move soon, else they'll be away.'

'What makes you think I'm interested?'

'You came here, didn't you?'

Yes, I did, thought Mike. I was looking for a traitor and found that the traitor was me.

'I came here to kill you,' said Mike.

'Good,' said Ratcliffe. He licked his lips. 'First things first, then.'

Ace was flung against the window as the Doctor threw the Bedford van round a corner. Up ahead she could see a burnt-out Dalek in the middle of the road.

'Dalek,' said Ace.

'What type?'

'Imperial, I think.' Ace hung on to the seat as the Doctor swerved round the broken casing. Debris crunched under the van's tyres. 'It's hard to tell.'

'Imperial,' said the Doctor. 'A scout model.'

'How can you tell?'

'Fairings are wider.'

'Oh.'

The Doctor changed gears and the van accelerated.

They turned another corner and Ace felt the rear wheels skidding. The van leaned over ominously, then straightened. A rail tunnel was dead ahead. Wrecked Daleks were clustered around its entrance, all of them in the cream and gold imperial livery.

The Doctor was forced to slow down to thread his way through them and into the tunnel. Smoke roiled around the ceiling.

'There was a major battle here,' said the Doctor.

'No kidding,' said Ace. 'I can't see any wrecked renegades.'

The Doctor slammed on the brakes; Ace was jerked forward. 'Watch it, Professor.'

The Doctor jumped out and crossed in front of the van. Ace slid back her door and followed. The Doctor was kneeling by two, oval patches of black on the road. He motioned Ace to stay back, and from his coat he pulled a device which he held over the nearest sooty patch. The device chattered violently and the Doctor snatched back his hand.

'Radiation?' asked Ace.

The Doctor nodded and switched off the device. It vanished back into his coat. 'And lots of it. That is all that is left of a couple of Daleks.' The Doctor looked up the road. 'I think the imperial Daleks have brought out their big guns.'

The special weapons Dalek punched a hole through the renegade central positions. Behind it, section four and the shuttle commander mopped up the survivors.

The renegade Daleks on the northern and southern

flanks were forced to withdraw. As they broke cover the imperial Daleks surged forward to cut them down.

The Emperor watched the white stars on the situation map dose in on the Renegade base. *How long before the Renegade's time corridor is established?*

Five minutes, reported Scan-op.

It was all a matter of time.

One part of the Dalek Supreme watched the two human captives. Another monitored the current tactical situation. Contact had been lost with all the front line warriors.

Departure in three minutes, reported the girl.

Instigate equipment destruct sequence, ordered the Dalek Supreme. *All warriors fall back to transit zone.*

The Bedford van swerved up on to the curb. Ace's head bounced against the van's roof. The Doctor stamped on the brake pedal; Ace flung out her arms to protect herself as she lurched forward.

'Out,' shouted the Doctor.

Ace slung back her door and jumped onto the pavement.

The Doctor rolled over the passenger seat, out of the door and landed on his feet beside her. He put his finger to his lips, then motioned for Ace to look over the bonnet.

Ace looked. Down the road she could make out the gates of Ratcliffe's yard. She heard a scraping noise to her left. Ace slowly turned her head. It was a Dalek –

or perhaps was once a Dalek. Instead of the normal manipulator arm and gunstick arrangement, a vast gun barrel sprouted from its torso. Flanges swept back from the gun's muzzle and terminated in concentric rings of metal. The Dalek was filthy. Grime streaked over its flanges and fairing.

Ace continued to watch as it went past the van towards Ratcliffe's yard. A phalanx of imperial Daleks followed. Ace ducked down behind the bonnet.

'Which blobs do you think are winning?' asked the Doctor.

'The bazooka blobs,' said Ace.

17
SATURDAY, 16:32

It happened very fast.

Mike and Ratcliffe were ushered outside by the Black Dalek. In the yard, grey Daleks were clustered closely round the Hand of Omega. The girl carried out the time controller and placed it on a trestle in front of the Hand of Omega. 'Time controller fully operational,' said the girl. 'Departure imminent.'

Too bad about Ratcliffe's plan, thought Mike.

The Black Dalek rotated to face the two men. 'Destroy human captives.'

'No!' shouted Ratcliffe.

The world shook: the yard gates dissolved into an orange ball of flame; heat washed the exposed skin of Mike's hands and face. Then the noise came, smashing him back against the double doors.

Mike saw Ratcliffe running for the time controller and the Black Dalek twisting to follow his path. A bolt of light hit the Dalek next to Mike; flame blossomed from its top dome. There was a ringing in his ears.

Ratcliffe snatched the time controller and shouted something.

More beams of light streaked through the smoke that masked the smashed gates. Another Dalek exploded. Mike saw the iron fire escape that ran up to the warehouse's second storey and lunged for it.

The Dalek Supreme was getting confusing sensory input. Images from the girl's eyes kept merging with its own optical sensors. It caught a fragmentary glimpse of Ratcliffe picking up the time controller. It tried to shoot, but the double image confused its fire control and the energy bolt went wide.

Incoming fire from the imperial Daleks was intensifying; the renegade Daleks' defence was disorganized.

The Dalek Supreme's options were limited. It spat an order at the girl. *Recover the time controller.*

The blast caught Ace and the Doctor half-way towards Ratcliffe's yard. Even at fifty metres Ace felt the heat of the fireball. She had been looking at the gates when they exploded, and her eyes were dazzled. Ace blinked, but all she could see was the orange after-image.

The Doctor took her by the hand and she stumbled after him.

Power crackled through the girl's nervous system. Charged as she was, time went slowly. She easily dodged the blaster bolts that seemed to float through the air. Her augmented eyes zeroed in on the human, Ratcliffe. In a moment she could see everything: the complex organic molecules that formed the fabric of his suit, the interplay of muscle in his shoulders, the constant motion of those absurdly fragile internal organs.

Power bunched up inside her; she flung out her arms

to Ratcliffe and loosed it.

Mike heard Ratcliffe stumble behind him. He turned to see Ratcliffe falling forward, crackling blue fire racing along his back. Ratcliffe's eyes were open in surprise, his mouth worked silently. He held out the burning globe of the time controller.

Mike took it as Ratcliffe fell to the iron steps. At the bottom of the fire escape Mike saw the girl. She was smiling.

The shuttle commander swung to the left of the special weapons Dalek. Its eyestick scanned the yard as it searched for the renegade Dalek Supreme. The shuttle commander took a glancing hit from a blaster bolt and lost three of its sensor globes.

Alarms sounded as the Abomination fired. The radiation discharge overwhelmed the shuttle commander's shields.

The shuttle commander saw a flash of black in its peripheral vision, and shot forward, compensating for the rough terrain by overloading its motivator.

The distinctive black casing of the Dalek Supreme was framed in the shuttle commander's aiming retide. The shuttle commander fired once but the Dalek Supreme shifted sideways and the shot missed.

It tried to line up again, but the Dalek Supreme had turned to bring its own weapon to bear. The shuttle commander's optical sensors whited out as a blaster bolt clipped its dome; it blindly returned fire. Its sight cleared just in time to see the Dalek Supreme vanish through the doorway to the warehouse.

The Abomination fired again and the last renegade was obliterated.

The shuttle commander's life support indicators were red-lining. It could feel vital systems shutting down as its power-plant ceased to function. With fading vision it looked at the Omega device – the imperial Daleks had triumphed.

Darkness closed in. With a final gurgling sigh the shuttle commander commended its database to the Empire. Then it died.

The systems co-ordinator relayed the data to the Emperor. *We have recovered the Omega device.*

18
SATURDAY, 16:34

'I can see again,' said Ace as she opened her eyes. She and the Doctor were opposite Ratcliffe's yard. Smoke obscured the interior but the firing had stopped.

'Which blobs won?' she asked.

Dalek shapes began to emerge from the smoke – the Doctor's hand tensed in her own.

'I don't know,' he said.

Wind began to shred the smoke. The Daleks were revealed: they were cream and gold imperial warriors. Ace felt the Doctor's hand relax. They watched as the Daleks moved out of the yard towards them.

'Professor,' said Ace.

'Oh,' said the Doctor, and pulled her backwards. She got a quick glimpse of the sign which read 'Beware of the Dog' before the Doctor slammed the door shut.

One thing about the Professor, thought Ace, is that he always has a getaway route handy.

There was a growl behind them.

Most of the time, she appended.

The Alsation growled again as they turned. Its lips were pulled back from its teeth, and a tiny strand of saliva trailed from its muzzle. Brown eyes stared at the Doctor. It snarled again. Ace could see its back legs tensing, hindquarters dipping in readiness to spring.

'Shush,' said the Doctor.

The Alsation's eyes grew puzzled. The tension left its body and its head drooped guiltily while its tail wagged in low, hopeful arcs.

Don't worry about it, dog, thought Ace, he has the same effect on me.

The Alsation trotted over to the Doctor's feet and rolled over on its back. 'Good dog,' said the Doctor, and bent over to rub its stomach.

The Dalek Supreme overrode the battle computer and instigated the equipment destruct program. The link with the girl was down, so the Dalek Supreme was able to think clearly for the moment. Energy reserves were dangerously depleted; combat would be unrealistic. As the last remaining Dalek of the renegade task-force it was imperative that it return home to report.

The Dalek Supreme triggered the destruct sequence and left the office. Behind it the battle computer burst into flames.

Mike stood completely still. The second floor of the warehouse was dark – he could just make out rows of shelves. He knew the creepy girl was in there with him because he had heard her light footsteps come through the doorway behind him. Now he listened in the darkness, waiting for her to make her move. His palm was slick on the handle of the pistol.

Mike smelled smoke. Now what? he thought.

He heard them – a patter footsteps over by the internal stairwell. If he could make it to the fire escape, if no Daleks were left in the yard and if the girl didn't catch him, he might get away.

And after that?

Mike figured he would worry about that later.

'The imperial Daleks have got the Hand of Omega,' said the Doctor. 'Good.'

Ace idly scratched the Alsatian's head. 'Why are you so keen that the Daleks should get it anyway?'

'Quiet, Ace,' said the Doctor. He opened the gate.

Ace left the dog and joined the Doctor.

A figure slipped out of the yard and started to trot up the road.

'It's Mike,' said Ace.

'He's got the time controller,' said the Doctor. 'Typical human, you can always count on them to mess things up.'

Thanks a lot, thought Ace.

'Ace, get after him, see where he's going and stay with him.'

'Right,' said Ace. She took off, but was momentarily restrained by the Doctor.

'And no heroics,' he said. 'I have enough problems already.'

'Trust me,' said Ace.

The Doctor watched Ace run up the street. Then he turned to look across at Ratcliffe's yard. The smoke had cleared now and the Doctor could see a body lying sprawled on the fire escape. It was George Ratcliffe – another death in a chain of blood that stretched from the future to the past.

I shall be well rid of the Daleks, thought the Doctor.

Something warm was butting him in the back of the knee. It was the Alsatian, snuffling for the Doctor's affection. He stroked the dog's head. 'I wonder who you remind me of.' The Doctor straightened, sighed and started back towards the van.

He had work to do.

19
SATURDAY, 16:45

The special weapons Dalek returned to the shuttle in triumph. Behind it floated the Hand of Omega. After the death of the shuttle commander the Abomination had assumed command. Pride filled the mutant as it boarded, the Emperor's benediction was a clear undercurrent within the encrypted command-net.

The Omega device was placed in the prepared storage module at the rear of the shuttle. The dead pilot was replaced by a warrior from section four. Even now the chosen Dalek's mind was filled with the relevant database, downloaded from the shuttle's computer.

The shuttle started to vibrate as the engines warmed up. The last of the Daleks filed aboard and started lock-down procedures. There were many empty spaces.

'What are you going to do when all this is over?' asked Allison.

Rachel thought for a moment. 'Retire to Cambridge and write my memoirs.'

'Professor?' Gilmore appeared at the top of the cellar stairs.

'Subject to security vetting of course,' said Rachel.

Gilmore came half-way down the stairs and called down to the two women. 'The shuttle appears to be leaving.'

Allison leapt to her feet. 'Good riddance to bad rubbish.'

She's as bad as Ace, thought Rachel. Was I like that when I was young? Did I just walk away from horror like that?

Suddenly she remembered a beach in August 1940 where the sun was going down in smoke. She could clearly see the stark angular shape of the radar towers against the sky. The sea was like a sheet of silver. She held him close, just to prove that they were both still alive. Yes we did – we spat death in the eye when we fought our war, she decided.

The four thrusters at the base of the shuttle roared. The concrete of the playground became white hot and burst into flame. The shuttle lifted on four pillars of smoke and fire, fighting to be free of the world. It rose slowly at first, then gathering speed it leaped for the sky.

The Doctor stood by the TARDIS and watched the shuttle accelerate into the upper atmosphere. He raised his hat as it departed.

Enjoy this moment, monsters, thought the Doctor. Enjoy the brief moment of flight as you soar high above this pathetic little world. Except, of course, you can't. You eradicated such worthless little pleasures centuries ago. The Doctor held on to that thought. It would make what he had to do easier.

Ace heard the rumble and looked up. A shadow passed over her face. The shuttle shot away high over the houses, the noise of its engines dopplered into the distance. Ace stopped and watched it vanish.

'Wicked,' she breathed.

Ace looked around to get her bearings. She was pretty certain that Mike was heading east, out of the evacuation zone, but where?

She jammed her hands into her coat pockets. Inside her left pocket she felt something small and metallic. Her thumb ran down a serrated edge. It was a door key. She took it out and looked at it. Then, putting her hands back in her pockets, Ace set off deeper into Shoreditch.

The girl was skipping. The road slipped away under her feet. The houses drifted past like smoke. The girl tracked the female target as she turned a corner. Probability assessment indicated that the female target would lead the girl to the male target. They were both marked for extermination.

A star burned deep in the heart of the *Eret-mensaiki Ska*, contained in a bottle of gravito-magnetic force. The interface stripped raw power from the plasma core and transformed it into electricity: one hundred and twenty-three million watts, usable, clean and versatile. Power to control; power to command.

Cables spread from the reactor to the thrusters and stardrive that gave the ship motion; to the life support plants that gave it life; to the sensors that gave it eyes; and to the batteries of weapons that gave the *Eret-mensaiki Ska* its teeth. Beside the cables ran a network of extruded glass. Through this network flashed digital instructions carried on the back of laser beams. The glass fibre nerves ran from every extremity, bunching at ganglia, thickening as they wound through the ship towards the hub. There they terminated at the centre of all commands – the bridge. And at the centre of the bridge was the Emperor – a white spider hanging in a silver web.

The Emperor oversaw the flight of the shuttle. Inside the bloated, round casing, data flickered through neural implants. If the Emperor had wished it, control of that flight could have been his if he willed it so.

Shuttle switching to docking mode, reported Tac-op.

On board the shuttle was the prize, the seminal device of the ancient Time Lords – the Hand of Omega. *What do you think of that, Doctor?* thought the Emperor. *I know that you are down there, on that pathetic little world. What desperate plan can your devious mind devise now?*

Vast doors in the belly of the mothership opened. With precise spurts of power the shuttle rose into the docking bay. The engines began to wind down. Multi-armed robots converged on its skin. A disembarkation corridor mated with the forward airlock.

Silent in the vacuum, the vast doors closed behind it.

20
SATURDAY, 17:15

'Well, Doctor,' said Gilmore, 'are we out of the woods yet?'

Rachel stepped aside to allow the Doctor past. He checked the connections that ran from the transmat to the television.

'Providing everything goes according to my plan,' said the Doctor.

Allison shuffled closer to watch the Doctor work. He ran his fingers over the camera on top of the television, then down the cable to the transmat. 'I don't suppose you could let us know what your plan is?' she asked.

'It's a surprise,' said the Doctor.

'Oh good,' said Rachel. 'I love surprises.'

The Doctor pulled a pair of tweezers from his coat and picked out a cable from the cabinet. He checked the end of the cable and frowned. He kicked the cabinet and looked at the cable, then at the cabinet. The Doctor lashed out with his foot: the transmat shook and a point of light appeared at the end of the cabinet. The Doctor straightened up, removed his hat and with a nervous little movement ran his fingers through his hair.

Rachel suddenly felt herself grow tense.

The Doctor replaced his hat and turned to face them. 'How do I look?' he asked. 'No, don't answer that.'

He turned back to the television and switched it on. As the set warmed up static filled the screen. The Doctor coughed once and brought the cable in the tweezers to his mouth.

'Calling Dalek mothership,' he said, 'come in, please.'

Rachel felt a hand touch her forearm.

The Doctor banged the top of the television. 'Dalek mothership, come in please.' The static slowly cleared.

The hand slipped into Rachel's – the skin was rough and warm. It was a man's hand. Group Captain Gilmore was standing close behind her; his uniform brushed her shoulder.

An image began to form on the screen. The cellar seemed to grow darker.

The image was blurred, showing ghosted objects. In the centre was a Dalek with a bloated dome. There was an impression of space around it and of purposeful activity. Gilmore's hand tightened on Rachel's.

'Ah,' said the Doctor, 'there you are.'

Rachel looked away from the screen and at the Doctor. Flickering light played across his face. His eyes were hard and bright. He seemed suddenly larger.

'This is the Doctor,' he said. 'President of the High Council of Time Lords, keeper of the legacy of Rassilon, defender of the Laws of Time and Protector of Gallifrey. I call upon you to surrender the Hand of Omega and return to your customary time and place.'

The misshaped Dalek on the screen shifted slightly. 'Ah Doctor,' it said. 'You have changed again, your appearance is as inconstant as your intelligence. You have confounded me for the last time.'

The bloated dome cracked open and slid back. Inside the Dalek shell was a creature whose head was cradled by metal braces from which wires trailed down into the hidden body of the Dalek shell. A face that had once been humanoid, but no longer. Its eyes were hollow scars, the skin of its cheeks was withered and cracked. Only its mouth moved, the lips twisting obscenely.

'Davros,' said the Doctor, 'I should have known.'

The Doctor's hated face filled the main viewing screen. Davros had always known that in the end it would come to this – a final confrontation between the Doctor and himself. Davros remembered all the times he had faced this meddling Time Lord, each defeat squirrelled away – every humiliation – to be brought out to make his victory sweeter.

Davros could feel the preparations falling into place.

Omega device locked in and running, reported the systems co-ordinator.

'I warn you, Davros,' said the Doctor, 'the Hand of Omega is not to be trifled with.'

Omega device prepared and standing by. All control systems are optimal. Time-space co-ordinates set in.

'I think I am quite capable of handling the technology, Doctor,' said Davros.

'I sincerely doubt that,' said the Doctor.

'Does it worry you, Doctor,' said Davros, 'that with it I can transform Skaro's sun into a source of unimaginable power?'

It worries me, thought Rachel, and I don't even know what he is talking about. She looked at the Doctor, but his face showed nothing.

'With that power at our disposal the Daleks will sweep away Gallifrey and its impotent quorum of Time Lords.' Davros's voice rose, a tinny shrieking from the television's speaker. 'The Daleks shall seize control of time itself, we shall become…'

'All powerful,' screamed the Doctor. Rachel flinched back, clinging on to Gilmore's hand to keep herself upright.

'Crush the lesser races, conquer the galaxy,' shouted the Doctor. 'Unimaginable power, unlimited rice-pudding and so on and so on.'

'Do not anger me, Doctor,' hissed Davros. 'I can destroy you and this miserable insignificant planet.'

'Wonderful,' said the Doctor. 'What power, what brilliance. You could wipe out the odd civilization, enslave the occasional culture.'

Rachel watched Davros thrashing with anger in his casing. She remembered the vast spaceship that hung above their heads – 'That ship, Group Captain, has weapons that could crack this planet like an egg.'

'But it won't detract from the fundamental truth of your own impotence,' said the Doctor. Davros's mouth hung open, uttering nothing but a gurgling sound. Rachel was suddenly very scared.

'Careful, Doctor,' she said.

The Doctor covered the microphone and turned to her. 'Trust me,' he said, 'I know what I'm doing.'

*

Davros rocked within his shell. He could feel his anger being smothered by the tranquillizers that were pumped in by his life support system. He knew he had defeated the Doctor, but it wasn't enough. The Doctor must be shown.

'I will teach you the folly of your words,' said Davros. 'I shall demonstrate the power of the Daleks.'

'Davros,' said the Doctor, 'I beg of you, do not use the Hand of Omega.'

'Now you begin to fear.'

'You're making a grave mistake,' said the Doctor.

Activate the Omega device.

'Now the Daleks will be the Lords of Time,' said Davros.

The Omega device felt the go-signal.

With a burst of power it howled out of the mothership and soared into space. Around it the space-time continuum blazed with shifting planes of force. Within moments the Hand of Omega had accelerated to near light speed – within minutes it had passed the orbit of Jupiter. There in transjovian space it found a nexus, a place where the fabric of space and time was malleable.

Gathering its strength the Hand of Omega lunged down and punched a hole in reality.

21

Skaro

It was dawn on the *Vekis Nar-Kangji*, the Plain of Swords – a wasteland of dust and bones bisected by a range of mountains. Here, twenty millennia ago, the final conflict between the Thals and Kaleds had ended.

Here in the ash-brown foothills of the mountains was the Dalek city, *Mensvat Esc-Dalek*. Light from the rising sun glanced off metal spires two thousand metres above the plain. Robot cargo-carriers took off and landed from hundreds of platforms, carving cybernetic flight patterns in the air and filling it with their ceaseless buzzing. The city's roots burrowed into the feet of the mountains.

The sun climbed off the horizon. Red light spilled across the plain. Yellow and black beetles scuttled into their nests. High in the stratosphere, streamers of cloud formed.

For a fragment of non-time, time was irrelevant and distance was a delusion. On the fringes of the Skarosian system the Hand of Omega became part of the normal universe.

In the mind of the device, only the star was significant. A great globe of hydrogen atoms moving at vast speeds – a dream where gravitational force fought with the star's impulse to expand into vacuum.

The device gloried in the mass of the star, its intensity and the frenzy of its interior. Like a dolphin, the device swam towards the core – the old cold core of iron and nickel that spun forever.

The device spread wings of force around the core and stopped for a heartbeat. In that heartbeat it doubled the gravitational flux. The Hand of Omega clenched the heart of the star in a fist of pure energy. The star began to collapse inwards, the fusion of hydrogen accelerated, and the pressure increased. The core began to degenerate: atoms were stripped of their electrons and forced together. The star became smaller, hotter and brighter.

Then the Hand of Omega let go.

The star died.

Under the Plain of Swords the beetles stirred in their nests. In the sky above, the sun changed. One thousand million Daleks stopped. The rock leopards in the mountains howled in terror. The sky turned white hot. One thousand million Daleks cried out in defiance.

Then the seas boiled, the metal cities of the Daleks ran like wax, and the atmosphere was blown away into space.

Skaro died.

The star convulsed and wrenched itself apart. Its outer crust blasted into an expanding globe of fire. The planets it had given life were vapourized one by one as the star bloated and ate its children.

Through it all passed the Hand of Omega, screaming its mirth. Then it shot back into the place that is no place on its way back to the past.

No, this cannot be correct, thought Davros, but the data was impossible to deny – the supernova and the cessation of signals from Skaro. And all the time the Doctor looked down from the main screen.

Omega device returning, impact minus twelve.

'You tricked me,' said Davros.

'No, Davros,' said the Doctor, 'you tricked yourself.'

Minus ten.

'Did you really think I'd let you have the Hand of Omega?' asked the Doctor.

'Do not do this, I beg of you.'

Minus nine.

'Nothing can stop it now.'

'Have pity on me.'

Minus eight.

'I have pity for you,' said the Doctor. 'Goodbye, Davros, it hasn't been pleasant.'

Minus seven.

The Doctor cut the connection. The main screen faded to black.

The Hand of Omega tore through the *Eret-mensaiki Ska*, ripping through armour and decks. All the energy it had collected from the supernova burst from it. The fusion heart that had driven the ship went critical.

The ship became a fireball which evaporated into space.

A small escape pod tumbled away, out of the Earth's orbit.

Inside, a single lifeform, deformed and bitter, cursed as the temperature of the pod's cabin fell towards zero.

Hate would keep him warm.

'What happened?' asked Rachel. The Doctor disconnected the cables and packed up the camera. Gilmore slowly let go of Rachel's hand.

'Oh,' said the Doctor, 'I programmed the Hand of Omega to fly into Skaro's sun and turn it supernova.'

'Super what?' asked Gilmore.

'He blew it up,' said Allison.

'The resulting feedback destroyed the mothership,' said the Doctor. 'The Hand of Omega is returning to Gallifrey.'

'You planned this all along,' said Rachel. 'Right from the start, it was all a trap.'

'Yes,' said the Doctor.

'We won,' said Gilmore. 'It's a victory.'

But the Doctor said nothing.

22
SATURDAY, 17:37

It was beginning to get dark by the time Ace reached Ashton Road. She jogged along the terrace looking into windows. A sign caught her eye. It read: 'NO BLACKS OR DOGS'. She found Mike's house. There were no lights in the windows.

Ace took the key from her pocket and turned the lock. There was no sound from the other side. She pushed open the door and stepped inside. Ace froze in the hallway, listening. The living room door was ajar. There was no noise.

I'd be a real wally to walk in there, she thought.

Ace took a deep breath and entered. The time controller was on the mantelpiece among Mrs Smith's knick-knacks.

'Hallo, Ace,' said Mike.

Ace turned slowly. Mike slowly closed the door. He was pointing a gun at her. Light from the streetlamp outside fell on him. Half his face was in shadow.

'Would you really shoot me?' asked Ace.

'If I had to,' said Mike.

'You might have to,' said Ace.

The girl walked down Ashton Road. This close, she could feel the radiated signature of the time controller.

It was in the habitation that the female target had just entered. There was a seventy-six per cent probability that the male target was with her.

A chilly breeze blew down the street.

The girl concentrated and sent her mind out to the Dalek Supreme.

The message struck the Dalek Supreme with unexpected force. *Time controller located,* reported the girl. The Dalek suddenly felt cold; its life support heating units stepped up.

Eliminate male and female targets and recover the time controller, ordered the Dalek Supreme and cut the link. The chill passed. The Dalek did a swift sensor-scan of the street. It registered no native activity. The Dalek Supreme moved out of Ratcliffe's yard.

It would meet the girl and use the time controller to return home. There it would make its report to the renegade council. Perhaps then it would be allowed to commit suicide.

Suicide? The Dalek recoiled from the alien thought. It checked the link with the girl. There was residual activity – the Dalek could not shut the mind-gate completely. Parts of the girl's personality continued to filter through.

There was activity at the extreme range of its sensors – the unmistakable output pattern of internal combustion engines. It swung its optical sensor round in an arc. Native transports were lumbering inelegantly towards it from both ends of the road.

At its depleted power levels the Dalek Supreme was incapable of sustained combat. The tactical computer assessment was bleak. The crude weapons of the humans would overwhelm it.

The Dalek Supreme prepared to make its last stand.

The doorbell rang.

'Stay there,' said Mike.

'It could be the Doctor,' said Ace as Mike stepped into the hallway. 'Put the gun down, Mike, it's too late for that.'

'Just stay there.'

'Come on, Mike, who're you going to shoot with it anyway?'

Gilmore brought the van to a halt and pointed down the road. Rachel craned to see past the Doctor in the front seat. A hundred yards away, in front of Ratcliffe's yard was a Dalek. Streetlamps cast highlights on its black livery.

One of the big Bedfords blocked the road behind it. Soldiers were beside the truck. They waited in the shadows, their weapons trained on the Dalek.

'This is the last Dalek,' said Gilmore. 'I'll call for reinforcements.'

'No,' said the Doctor, 'not this time.' He slammed back the van door and got out. 'I started this…'

The doorbell rang continuously. Mike tucked the gun into his belt, out of sight behind his back. Mike reached for the doorknob. The ringing stopped. He could see a shadow on the stained glass of the front door. It was small, like a child. Mike opened the door.

The girl stood on the porch.

For a moment Mike stood frozen in confusion. It cost him his life. He recognized the girl. She worked for the Daleks, and was somehow almost like a Dalek herself.

Mike reached for his gun. The girl flung up her arms, hands curved like talons. Mike's hand closed round the pistol butt.

Blue light seared his eyes, he felt himself smashed backwards into the bannisters. Wood splintered. There was a moment of agony before everything faded to black.

Now I'll finish it, thought the Doctor.

He walked towards the Dalek, which swivelled to face him.

'Dalek,' he called, 'you have been defeated. Surrender – you have failed.'

'Insufficient data.'

It was strange, this impulse among organic intelligences to turn themselves into machines and ape the form and mannerisms of robots. Daleks, Cybermen and Sontarans all sought perfection, but what did they find in the end?

'Your forces are destroyed, and the planet of your birth is a burnt cinder circling a dead sun.'

'There is no data.'

In the end they found nothing – nothing at all.

Ace flinched as blue light filled the doorway. There was a sharp smell of ozone. In the corner the television set turned itself on. Ace backed away from the doorway –

the back of her knees banged into the sofa. The lightbulb overhead flared into double brightness, then shattered. Glass cut her cheek. Tinny music began to blare from the radio on the ironing board.

The girl stood in the doorway. In the flickering light of the television screen, Ace could see the girl's eyes glitter.

'You will have no more commands from your superiors,' said the enemy of the Daleks, 'because you have no superiors.'

The Dalek Supreme could feel the triumph leaking through from the girl. It was like a whirlwind battering at the Dalek's mind, and at the storm's eye, the Dalek could feel an icy bleakness.

Ace saw the girl move and threw herself backwards. Energy crackled over her as she tumbled over the back of the sofa. Glass shattered over the mantelpiece.

If you are going to lie, thought the Doctor, make it a big one.

'No inferiors,' he told the Dalek, 'no reinforcements, and no hope of rescue. You are trapped a trillion miles and a thousand years from a disintegrated home.'

He watched the Dalek carefully. Its gunstick twitched and its eyestalk described tiny circles in the air. Easy does it, thought the Doctor and stepped closer.

'I have annihilated the entire Dalek species,' he said.

The whirlwind of the girl's emotions stormed the ramparts of the Dalek Supreme's mind. A lifetime's conditioning, from incubator to the present, was swept away by a child's despair.

For a microsecond, the girl and the Dalek became one personality, both in the room of the house and both in the road outside Ratcliffe's Yard. The girl shared the taste of power of the killings done under alien skies. The Dalek Supreme was assailed by the moment of birth, the scream of the newborn, the warm comforting arms of the female.

The commonality of mind and purpose that is the Dalek race.

The isolation and loneliness that is the human being.

The Dalek thrashed in its life support chamber, random neural spurts shot through its control systems. A logic gate closed. A failsafe was bypassed. The remaining power reserves were released.

The Dalek Supreme exploded.

Ace was hiding behind the sofa when she heard the girl scream.

It went on for a long time, rising over the noise of the radio. Then it stopped. The radio went quiet. The television turned off. It went very quiet. Ace tried to catch her breath.

Then she heard it. A low whimpering sob, the hiss of an indrawn breath and then another sob. The sofa quivered. In the darkness, the girl was crying.

Ace got to her feet and walked around the sofa. In the light from the hallway she could see the girl curled into a tight ball on the cushions. Ace sat down and took the girl in her arms. Through the doorway she could see

Mike's legs. They lay unmoving on the lino floor.

'It's all right,' she told the girl, 'it's all over now.'

The girl buried her face in Ace's shoulder and wept. The tears were easier and cleaner now. Ace looked away from the doorway and began to cry with her.

Nothing was left of the Dalek Supreme but ashes. Efficient to the last, thought the Doctor as he looked down on the remains. From nothing you came, to nothing you aspired, to nothing you went.

'Ashes to ashes,' said the Doctor, 'dust to dust.'

May you rest in pieces forever.

23
Thursday, 11:30

Dear Julian,

How are you? Just dropping a note to say I'm all right. It's been five days since the excitement stopped and I suppose things are getting back to normal.

The Doctor disappeared with that creepy little girl shortly after we found her and Ace at Mike's house. He brought her back yesterday and Gilmore's got people looking for her parents now.

When I asked him what he'd been doing, all he said was 'rewiring'. I didn't ask him to elaborate – to be honest I'm not sure I wanted to know.

Rachel and Gilmore have been in each other's company a lot. He calls her Rachel and she calls him Ian. I think they might have something going, but their faces seem so melancholy now.

Ace and I have been left to twiddle our thumbs here at Maybury Hall. Sometimes when she talks I don't understand half the things she says. It frightens me a little. If she really is from twenty-five years in the future then our children could grow up to be like her.

Must dash – we're burying poor old Mike Smith today. He won't get military honours, but Gilmore said we all had to go anyway. The funeral is at the same cemetery where the Doctor buried the Hand of Omega, which I think is a bit of a coincidence, but the Doctor says it's just the stitching in the fabric of reality showing at the seams. Hope to see you soon.

Love Allison.

This letter has been censored by order of the D-notice committee.

Six professional bearers carried Mike's coffin up the path to the church. Mrs Smith clung to Gilmore's arm, she was the only one crying. Behind them walked an elderly couple, introduced to Rachel as Mike's uncle and aunt. Rachel and Allison walked behind them; Ace and the Doctor brought up the rear. Nobody else came.

Mrs Smith seemed to have trouble walking.

She lost her husband and now her only son, thought Rachel. All she has are her memories. On Remembrance Sunday will she sit by the radio and remember her son, who died on the wrong side of a war that never officially happened? What will I remember in twenty years' time? As I watch the world rush headlong into the future, the world of the young, Ace's world. A silver sea in 1940, the Dalek at Totters Lane, the spaceship landing in the playground perhaps? Or will it be Turing stammering out his theories or Ian's warm hand on mine while we watched the Doctor engineer an act of genocide?

In the end that's all we have: our memories – electrochemical impulses stored in eight pounds of tissue the consistency of cold porridge. In the end they define our lives.

The Doctor put his hand on Ace's shoulder before they went into the church. 'Time to leave,' he said.

Ace looked into the Doctor's grey eyes.

'Yes,' she said. 'Doctor?'

'Yes?'

'We did good, didn't we?'

'Perhaps,' said the Doctor. 'Time will tell – it always does.'

Next in the *Doctor Who 50th Anniversary Collection:*

EARTHWORLD

JACQUELINE RAYNER

ISBN 978 1 849 90520 6

The Doctor Who *50th Anniversary Collection*
Eleven classic adventures
Eleven brilliant writers
One incredible Doctor

Anji has just had the worst week of her life. She should be back at her desk, not travelling through time and space in a police box. The Eighth Doctor is supposed to be taking her home, so why are there are dinosaurs outside? The Doctor doesn't seem to know either, or else he surely would have mentioned the homicidal princesses, teen terrorists and mad robots? One thing is certain: Anji is never going to complain about Monday mornings in the office again.

An adventure featuring the Eighth Doctor, as played by Paul McGann, and his companions Fitz and Anji.

DOCTOR WHO
The Encyclopedia

Gary Russell

Available for iPad
An unforgettable tour of space and time!

The ultimate series companion and episode guide, covering seven thrilling years of *Doctor Who*. Download everything that has happened, un-happened and happened again in the worlds of the Ninth, Tenth and Eleventh Doctors.

◊

Explore and search over three thousand entries by episode, character, place or object and see the connections that link them together

◊

Open interactive 'portals' for the Doctor, Amy, Rory, River and other major characters

◊

Build an A-Z of your favourites, explore galleries of imagery, and preview and buy must-have episodes